ELMHURST PUBLIC LIBRARY

3 1135 0192

P9-CLS-317

J F
HOLCZER

The
Secret Hum
of a
Daisy

Tracy Holczer

G. P. Putnam's Sons
An Imprint of Penguin Group (USA)

G. P. Putnam's Sons
Published by the Penguin Group
Penguin Group (USA) LLC
375 Hudson Street
New York, NY 10014

USA | Canada | UK | Ireland | Australia
New Zealand | India | South Africa | China
penguin.com
A Penguin Random House Company

Copyright © 2014 by Tracy Holczer.
Penguin supports copyright. Copyright fuels creativity, encourages diverse
voices, promotes free speech, and creates a vibrant culture. Thank you for
buying an authorized edition of this book and for complying with copyright
laws by not reproducing, scanning, or distributing any part of it in any form
without permission. You are supporting writers and allowing Penguin to
continue to publish books for every reader.

Library of Congress Cataloging-in-Publication Data
Holczer, Tracy.
The secret hum of a daisy / Tracy Holczer.
pages cm
Summary: "After 12-year-old Grace's mother's sudden death, Grace is forced to
live with a grandmother she's never met. Then she discovers clues in a mysterious
treasure hunt—one that will help her find her true home"—Provided by publisher.
[1. Moving, Household—Fiction. 2. Home—Fiction. 3. Grandmothers—Fiction.
4. Treasure hunt (Game)—Fiction. 5. Death—Fiction.] I. Title.
PZ7.H6974Sec 2014
[Fic]—dc23
2013039962

Printed in the United States of America.
ISBN 978-0-399-16393-7
3 5 7 9 10 8 6 4 2

Design by Annie Ericsson.
Text set in Horley Oldstyle.

To Kate, Sara, and Maddy
for showing me what it's all about

Where the bird was before it flew,
Where the flower was before it grew,
   Where bird and flower were one and the same.

—Robert Frost

1

Two Hundred
and Fifty-Six
Mississippis

All I had to do was walk up to the coffin. That was all.
I just had to get there and set the gardenia on the smooth
brown wood. Grandma said gardenias were a proper funeral flower. As if there was such a thing.

But my mind kept turning to daisies. The wild ones
I'd found and stuck into the cold white funeral wreaths.
Mama would have liked that. She'd told me that daisies
spoke in a kind of song, a secret humming that birds could
feel in their hollow bones, drawing them close. She said I
could feel it, too, if I tried, along the fine hairs of my arms
and neck. That we all have a little bird in us somewhere.

But there wasn't any bird in me. I could never hear the
daisies either. Or any other flower for that matter.

Listen, Grace. Mama's voice seemed to drift near the
stained glass windows where wet snow stuck and then slid
down the colored panes.

Grandma told me it had been a cold winter and it
wasn't over yet, even though it was April. One of the only

facts she'd shared with me since we'd met the week before. Of course, it wasn't like I knew how much it snowed here or when, being from just about everywhere else. In all our wandering across the great state of California, Mama had never mentioned the Sierra Nevadas or her hometown, Auburn Valley.

Grandma took my hand in her damp one and squeezed. Hard. "Listen, now," she said.

I pulled my hand out of hers with a juicy *plop* and wiped it down my skirt.

". . . she was a loving mother," said Pastor Dave, his voice turning from buzzing to words. More words like "free spirit," "quick to laugh," "full of life." Grandma fidgeted in her seat. Other people fidgeted too. I wondered if they'd known Mama years ago.

Then Pastor Dave said God took her for his own reasons.

But it wasn't God; it was the river.

I closed my eyes and pushed those thoughts away. Thoughts about Mama's last night, what I might have done different. Thoughts about Mrs. Greene and Lacey and how they were more of a family to me than Grandma would ever be. I turned around to find them at the back of the church, still fuming at Grandma for not letting them sit here in the front row with us. But just the sight of Mrs.

Greene, her quick nod of confidence, gave me the courage to do what I had to do.

Pastor Dave stopped talking when I stood up.

I stared down at my too-tight Mary Janes, skin puffing around the edges like marshmallow. Twelve was too old for those dumb shoes, but they were the only decent ones I owned. They squeaked as I stepped toward the giant sprays of sweet white flowers, eyeing the wild daisies I'd tucked in around the bottom.

There was a gasp. Or maybe it was my shoes.

Pastor Dave cleared his throat and picked up where he'd left off. Pews creaked, nylons hushed. I felt eyes on my back like a heat. I turned around to face those eyes, to look at Grandma, hard as the bench she sat on, daring her to stop me, but she was staring at Jesus in the stained glass window, her unused handkerchief held firmly in both long-fingered hands.

I picked the daisies out of the sprays. One by one by one. Heart thumping, I sat down on the red carpeted steps and made a daisy chain, weaving the stems in and out, in and out, reminding me of the number 8 and how Mama said we were like that, winding around and through each other, not sure where one picked up and the other left off. Pastor Dave must have given up on his speech because he stopped talking again, and after a short silence, the organist started "In the Garden," which I recognized from one of Mrs. Greene's Elvis records. Everyone stood, a commotion of creaking wood and turning pages, like they were glad for some direction.

I set the daisy crown right on top of the closed coffin lid, where Mama's head rested underneath, and then walked past Grandma, past all those other people who were studying their hymnals, singing for dear life. Right past Mrs. Greene, who reached out her hand so that I could brush mine against it, palm to palm.

The singing quieted as the door shut behind me. I sat down on the cold concrete steps under the eaves and watched the slush come down. "One Mississippi, two Mississippi, three Mississippi . . ." Drowning out the never-ending hymn.

Lacey followed and sat next to me, quiet. She took my hand in hers, our fingers intertwined like a chocolate-and-vanilla swirl. I leaned my head on her shoulder.

"Sisters forever," she said.

I couldn't make a sound, so I just nodded.

It took Grandma two hundred and fifty-six Mississippis to come outside. I didn't care it took her so long, though. Because I had a mama who never would have let me get past ten. We knew how to save each other.

2

Birds of Sorrow

Mama said she started living the day I was born, and when I was little, I took that as the literal truth. It was only ever the two of us, so I figured the stork dropped us down as a pair. The very first picture in our family photo album was of her, sitting up straight in the white sheets of a hospital bed, looking down at my little pink face and curly brown hair like she couldn't quite figure out where I came from but she was happy just the same. No childhood pictures of her. None of her pregnant. Just her and me in that hospital bed, dropped down together from some kind of heaven.

When I got to school, of course, I saw that most people had all manner of relatives. I didn't have to change my theory much, though. I decided that me and Mama were alone because the other pieces of our family broke off somewhere on the way down, and if Mama kept moving us around like she did, we'd run into them somewhere.

By that time I was seven and had been telling anyone who asked about my theories on the stork and my lost family. But it wasn't until second grade, when I gave Christopher Wales a black eye for telling me I was bonkers, that Mama finally cleared things up.

She was working on a junk-art bird at the kitchenette table in our tiny apartment, her long blond hair held back with a clip. Where I always managed to hang out my tongue or squinch my eyes when I was concentrating, Mama's face was still and pretty. She'd been building junk-art birds, mostly cranes, since before I was born. Making those birds was a cross between pure love and a nervous habit, the way some might do crossword puzzles or needlepoint. She sold them in the restaurants where she worked or at small flea markets and coffee shops for a little extra money. I thought they were the most beautiful creatures I'd ever seen and always felt a twinge when they flew away to their forever home, wishing we'd find ours.

She patted the metal folding chair next to her and smiled at me, a closed-lipped smile that hid a crooked tooth. As she went back to work inserting the rivets that closed the small metal body of the bird, she tried to explain a little about how babies come and that I'd had a daddy and grandparents once. I didn't want to believe her. My Stork Theory had been with me so long, it was almost like a friend.

But curiosity about the rest of my family won out.

"Where are they?" I said.

"Your daddy and grandpa died before you were born."

She stopped her riveting and swallowed a bunch of times, like their dying was caught in her throat. It stopped me, too, having to give up the idea of them so soon.

Mama toyed with the pile of spoons she always found a way to work into her birds. The late-afternoon sun shone its slanted light through the window, the winter dirt on the outside stealing some of its shine.

She went on to tell me they'd died together in a car accident, that my daddy had loved me every bit as much as she did. She walked to her dresser and brought out a small framed photo of her sitting in a patch of wild daisies next to a young man who had my high forehead and lopsided smile. His name was Scott. Then she picked up the slim volume of Robert Frost poetry she'd been reading to me every night since I was born. *A Boy's Will,* it was called.

"This is all I have left of him." He didn't have a family, she said. They'd died in a house fire when he was sixteen.

"What about Grandma?" I said, hopeful.

Mama sighed. She told me they had always fought like cats and dogs, and that her being young and pregnant was just too much for Grandma. She wasn't one to face things, Mama said, and so Grandma sent Mama on a bus to live with another family in Texas, "until they could figure out what to do next." Mama got off the bus in San Diego, California, and she'd been looking for the perfect home for us ever since.

It didn't occur to me right away that Grandma must be a horrible person, someone I wouldn't want to know. All I thought about was the idea that there was someone out there connected to me by blood. Someone we might belong to besides each other.

So I fired questions at Mama. Did you ever get along with Grandma? Where does she live? What did you and Grandma fight about? Do you think we'll ever see her? Why doesn't she come find us?

Mama took my face in her small hands and told me that thinking about where she came from was painful for her, even still. And I didn't want to be paining her, now, did I? "Because we take care of each other, right?" she said.

"But Grandma's still out there somewhere?"

"Yes."

"Doesn't she want to know where we are?" I swallowed hard. "Or who I am?"

Mama pulled me into her lap and her yellow chair creaked under our weight. "You have to trust me, Grace. We don't need anyone else."

So I believed her. Plus, I didn't want to add to her pains by bringing it up all the time. It seemed to me that

Grandma must have been a pretty terrible mother to send her own daughter packing while she was so young and pregnant. That made her mean. Small-minded. I decided right then and there she wasn't worth a speck of love.

Mama set me back on my chair. Then she went to the same dresser where she kept the picture of my father and took out a black-and-white-checked notebook. She set it on top of the Robert Frost book.

"Here," she said. "Sometimes it helps to write about things that make you sad."

I eyed her skeptically. "You're just trying to trick me into writing practice."

She laughed and the dark mood lifted.

"You caught me."

But I figured it couldn't hurt. So I wrote down some wobbly seven-year-old words.

Fly away sad feelings.

Each of her birds held a sorrow or a wish—all her sleepless nights and worries, all her hopes for the future—formed into words and sketches tucked deep inside those birds and meant to fly away. Before that day, I didn't know what she might be worried about, what might have made her feel sorrowful. I only understood my own sorrows, the way they would settle into the empty spaces meant to be filled by other things—a father, a place to call home—and I didn't know how to scrape them out.

Mama offered to let me tuck my words into the bird she was working on. But I wanted to keep them. They were mine. I wrote down more words that day, and most days since.

That was how I saved myself.

3

Just Like That

The sheriff's car led the funeral procession—patrol lights flashing against the world—turned left, and climbed a winding road to a small, unfenced cemetery. The cars parked around us, closing us in. People walked in small groups under giant black umbrellas.

Grandma informed me there wouldn't be a gathering afterward. One by one, the people who had attended stopped and gave a kind word but moved along quickly, as though they didn't know her any better than I did. There was one exception: an older lady in a worn straw cowboy hat, a faded leather jacket with fringe, and a black muumuu. She gave Grandma a long, fierce hug. Grandma surprised me by returning it. Margery was her name.

"You come visit me in town," she said to me. "I've got the hosiery shop. It's called Threads."

Before I could say a word, she'd walked away, dabbing her eyes with a red bandana.

Mrs. Greene and Lacey hung back and waited until everyone else had left. The four of us all faced one another.

"We'll come visit in a couple of weeks, before you go back to school," Mrs. Greene said. The black dress looked all wrong. Her usual choice of colors tended to compete with fire hydrants or October leaves.

Lacey squeezed my hand again and gave me a quick hug, her damp cheek pressing against mine.

After they left, I watched the coffin lower, forever it lowered, the crown of daisies balanced on top. Something in me needed to see it through even though the rest of me pulsed *run, run, run.* I looked up into the sky and wondered about heaven. If it was a big empty space or if there were all kinds of comfy chairs placed in small groups so new people wouldn't be overwhelmed. I pictured Mama sipping Earl Grey, stirring honey with one of her beloved spoons, her pale hair glowing in heaven's light, planning her next bird. I wondered if her back ached where her wings were coming in the way my legs ached when I'd had that growth spurt in fifth grade. If she might feel my thoughts and send some back.

"I'm sorry, Mama," I whispered.

I reached under the tarp covering all that dug-up earth around the hole, took a handful, and put it in the pocket of the peacoat of Mama's I'd taken to wearing. Then I took another handful for good measure. It started to slush again, and my outsides turned as numb as my insides. Grandma stood beside me, our black umbrellas tapping each other.

"Why did you want a crane on her headstone?" Grandma asked.

Mama used to leave me treasure hunts. She'd always start with a junk-art crane, where she'd tuck something safely inside, maybe a paper clip, which would lead me to the desk, where I'd find a key ring to the laundry room, and so on. Along the way I'd meet the people in her new job, the librarian, someone at the nearest market or video store. She'd have me going for a good three hours every time we moved. Her way of showing me around the new town and introducing the people in it. My very own treasure hunt where the final clue would always lead back to our new front porch, where Mama would wrap me in her arms and say we were each other's treasure.

I wasn't going to tell Grandma about the birds Mama used to make, or how the crane was her happiest bird, the one she always used for treasure-hunt clues. She could just stand there and wonder.

Eventually I figured there was no use dragging things out, so without a word to Grandma or the men standing by with their shovels, I turned and headed for the truck. Grandma followed close behind.

Most everything I had left in the world sat under a tarp

in the back of the pickup. Until we got to Mrs. Greene's, Mama had treated our moves like we were climbing into a hot air balloon, and we had to leave most everything behind in order to be light enough to float away.

The nylon rope was wet and splintery as I made sure the tarp was still tight over the bed of the truck. A broken plastic thread from the rope stabbed the palm of my hand. It bled.

Grandma unlocked the rusted handle on the passenger side, and then dug two handkerchiefs out of her giant black purse, giving one to me. The other she used to blow her nose. I waited for her to move before climbing in, holding the handkerchief tight in my fist.

When she got into the truck, she fished around in her purse again and came up with a Safeway plastic grocery bag. She nodded toward my pockets and set the bag on the seat between us.

"For the dirt," she said.

Mama died six days ago, and Grandma had tried to pick me up twice before, but I'd hidden from her. The threat of missing Mama's funeral was what finally made me get into her truck. At least twenty times per day, I'd begged Mrs. Greene to let me stay. But Mrs. Greene had said the same thing each time. "She's your grandma, Grace. You have to give it time. Everyone deserves a bit of time."

"What about what I deserve?"

"You deserve to be loved. But sometimes, you can't see what that looks like for yourself. You've got too much mad mixed up in there. Too much sorrow. After a few months, things will be different." Mrs. Greene had put her hand on my leg and squeezed, holding tight longer than was necessary.

Mama and I had lived with Mrs. Greene and Lacey for nine months, the longest we'd lived anywhere, and by the time we got there, I was tired. Tired of this adventure Mama said we were on, trying to find the perfect place to call home. For Mama, there was always a better job or a better place to live, better schools or less crime. A place with trees or, when she was sick of trees, a place with open fields or water or whatever it was that Mama needed to keep her spirits up. Mama told me that when we finally found home, it would hum. Like the daisies.

I thought we'd finally found that place when we found Mrs. Greene. The wide and slow movement of the Sacramento River was a quick walk from Mrs. Greene's back steps. The mountains were an hour's drive, and the beach was just a little farther in the other direction. Mrs. Greene had taken us under her wing, both me and Mama, into a safe place that felt like home. But things always seemed to happen at some point or another to make Mama want to leave, and Mrs. Greene's ended up being no different.

Grandma drove down Main Street, past the small church we'd just left and the public school next to it. As we drove past the snow-globe storefronts, I saw a giant spoon hanging from a pole in front of a restaurant called the Spoons Souperie. I spun around in my seat and watched the spoon swing in the wind.

"What is it?" Grandma said.

"Nothing."

Mama had used spoons in all of her birds, claiming that a spoon was the utensil of comfort. She said it brought you soup on a cold day and stirred honey in your tea. Without spoons we couldn't eat pudding or ice cream, and you could never hang a fork from your nose or ears.

It confused me to think she might have been using them because they reminded her of home. Home being a place she never talked about.

Thinking that was a question I couldn't answer, I let it go as we came to a four-way stop where the land opened to rolling fields and cedars. There was a sign welcoming us to Gold Country, California. One of the only other pieces of information Grandma had shared with me was that Auburn Valley was on the National Register of Historic Places because of how much gold had been discovered here. She explained it was an even smaller town now than it was then because of some fires that had burned the place down a long time ago.

After a short distance, she made a left on Ridge Road. She drove so slow, I almost could have walked faster.

Try as I might to picture the house where Mama had lived, the only picture I came up with was the witch's cottage from "Hansel and Gretel." As much as I'd like to see Grandma as the witch in that cottage, she was actually pretty ordinary looking. No tinge of green or warts. Instead, she had silver hair with streaks the same blond as Mama's pulled back into a loose knot, and she wore long gray skirts and tall black boots with flat heels, which didn't do anything to hide the length of her legs. She had a tiny silver cross at her neck, the only delicate part of her, it seemed, and a habit of touching it, like it was a raft floating in the middle of our wide and deep silences.

I'd written letters to Grandma when I was eight. Forbidden letters. The only thing in my life I kept secret from Mama. The letters started from a school assignment where we had to write to our grandparents. I asked questions you might ask a grandmother. How to make pie, for instance. Or knit. I was forever seeing grandmas out there making pie and knitting, and figured I had a right to know. There were plenty of angry letters too. I asked how she could turn her back on her own child, pregnant at seventeen.

I'd written a total of twenty-seven letters and bundled them with string like a miniature stack of newspapers. I still carried them from place to place in my army duffel.

"There'll be some house rules, of course," Grandma said as we drove. Her voice was low and husky like Mama's.

I continued to look out the foggy window.

"Certain rooms are off-limits. Your Grandpa's office right off the kitchen, my room. The kitchen is free to use as long as you clean up after yourself."

We passed a large wooden sign with letters branded into it that read BRANNIGAN. In the distance beyond the fence were two horses, one dark brown and the other whitish gray with darker gray splotches, like a stormy sky. They grazed, tails flapping. The gray one lifted her head and looked at us. She was beautiful, with a big round belly. Endless amounts of grass will do that to a horse, I figured.

Just past the horses, Grandma slowed and turned into a curved gravel driveway. Along the left edge, sun-bleached fence posts strung with rusted wire kept tall weeds from escaping a pasture, and the house sat at the top of a slight hill up ahead. There was a broken-down barn in the pasture, and a sturdy shed sitting off to the right. A thin metal smokestack poked out the top. Mama's and my car, Daisy, was parked beside it.

"Your sofa is in there," Grandma said.

"Is that your garage?"

"Used to be your grandfather's workshop."

I'd found a picture of Grandpa once, in one of Mama's

dresser drawers. He had silver and black hair, a big smile, and clearly loved the little girl who sat on his lap. Mama came into the room as I was looking at it, and took it carefully out of my hands. She told me three things before she put it away.

1. She loved Grandpa almost as much as she loved me.
2. He could build anything from a birdhouse to a skyscraper.
3. He was a birder and took her everywhere he went in search of rare birds.

She said that putting her junk-art birds together was her way of remembering.

Mama never told me anything about Grandma except the fact that she'd sent her away when Mama had needed her most. I supposed she figured that was enough.

Grandma drove up the gentle climb of the driveway and stopped in front of the house. There were two stories with attic windows on top, peeling sky-blue paint with white trim, also peeling, and a wood porch with two chairs covered in yellowed plastic and pine needles. Brass numbers hung on the front porch post, the middle number missing. I could tell from the tarnished outline that it had been the number 4. Piles of Tupperware and glass dishes covered in foil were set neatly beside the front door, a stack of firewood next to that.

Grandma sighed. I climbed out of the truck, thinking about the impossibility of eating, when I heard it. It was coming from behind the house. Distant and soft.

I couldn't help but follow the sound, through the backyard garden, which looked like something from a magazine with its rock walls and graceful trees. I walked fast, then ran toward the thick forest at the back. The gray horse I'd seen in the front pasture was running along the fence line beside me and stopped as I went into the trees.

"Where in heaven's name . . . ," Grandma called from somewhere behind me.

Her words faded as the sound of water got louder. I moved through the thick trees, ankle deep in pine needles, their sharp points biting through my tights. There was a clearing. Then the river.

It moved fast, sticks and torn branches rushing by. As I edged closer to the slippery rocks, I saw blond hair floating. Mermaid hair. Then gone. I sat down in a heap on the sand, trying to force the pictures out of my mind, but they played like a movie.

A policeman putting a wool blanket around my shoulders, trying to take Mama's hand from mine. How it took two of them to get me away from her. My hair dripping onto the scratchy wool of the blanket as I finally slumped against the policeman, resting my head on his shoulder. The edge of his badge in my ribs. How they asked me so many questions about what happened, and I couldn't answer. Then I wouldn't. I would never talk about that day.

Grandma crouched beside me. Words tumbled around my mind, and I itched for my notebook and pencil, but they were in the duffel in the bed of Grandma's truck.

"It must have been . . . awful."

"Is this the Sacramento River?" I said.

"It's called the Bear up here."

There was nothing else to do but stand up on wobbly legs and get away from the river, wet branches slapping me in the face and neck as I ran back through the woods.

Eventually, Grandma came around the house behind me, white mist puffing from her nose and mouth. She reached out a leather-gloved hand, but settled it on the rusted edge of the truck bed for support. She touched the cross at her neck.

Mama had spent my lifetime staying away from this person. She'd gotten herself off a bus in a place she didn't know and trusted a world of strangers could take better care of her than her own mother. I wasn't about to do anything different.

I paced beside the truck. "Mama said you sent her away, that you turned your back on us a long time ago."

Silence.

"I know it's true. I want to hear you say it."

Grandma took forever to answer. "Yes. I sent her away."

I stopped pacing. "Just like that?"

"Nothing is just like that."

I went to work untying the rope holding down the tarp. I took one last look at the house, picked up the closest box, and headed toward Grandpa's workshop.

4

Getting Stuck
That Way

Later that night, Grandma made threats about my staying in Grandpa's shed, but we didn't know each other well enough for them to have teeth. Short of slapping a padlock on the door, there wasn't a thing she could do. She must have figured it out, too, because after getting rid of a few old containers of paint thinner, a saw blade, and two rat traps, she took her tall self out the door and left me alone.

The workshop wasn't a bad place to stay. There was a wood stove in the corner to keep me warm. Sort of. But at least I knew how to keep it running from the six months I'd had in King City with the Girl Scouts. A bucket took care of the drip from the ceiling. There were glass jars lined along the back wall that held nuts and bolts and other metal doodads in case I needed to fix something. It smelled like wood chips and oiled hinges. I didn't care, though. As long as I had Mama's quilt and sofa, I could stay out here forever.

Best of all, I couldn't hear the river.

Trying to ignore the blasts of rain against the tin roof, I dug a flashlight out of one of the boxes and laid my sleeping bag and pillow on our flower-garden sofa. I took my latest notebook out of my duffel and climbed into the sleeping bag.

I hadn't written anything in the six days since Mama died, and the words were scratching at me in the way they always did. I hoped to find the end of that string inside myself—the string that tended to work itself into knots—and pull it straight. That was how the words felt sometimes as I wrote them down. Like I was taking something scrambled and unscrambling it.

My need for words was because of Mama. Not only did she give me my first journal, but every night of my life, as I'd drift off to sleep, she'd whisper Robert Frost poems into the quiet. I mostly didn't understand what the poems meant, but the rhythms gave me a feeling of comfort and they made me want to come up with my own sets of words. Mama told me I knew a lot for a kid, having moved around as much as we had, and that it was the living more than the poetry that made me smart. The last couple of years, she looked a little sad when she said it, like she wished my smarts had come a different way.

I settled back on the sofa and tried to let my mind drift toward something good. Something that might give me a few minutes of comfort. As I closed my eyes, though, the only thing I could see was Mama when I found her, and I would never write about that. Not ever.

It felt like the knots inside were about to cut off my circulation, so I read the last entry in my composition book to give me a place to start.

Riding the Bus

The smell of plastic seats
and Mr. Jenkins whistling like a bird
instead of saying hello,
his mustache curving around puckered lips.
Which made Lacey and me giggle
every time
because we couldn't picture
a Mrs. Jenkins smooching those lips.
We'd walk to the middle of the bus
making small kissing sounds
against the backs of our hands
while Mr. Jenkins' birdcall
followed us into the smooth green seat.
A good way to start the day.

It was weird to think how the girl who wrote that was gone. Like so gone, I could put up a missing-person poster. Then I realized all ten of my notebooks were Before, and what I was about to write would be After.

I couldn't do it. I wouldn't talk about it or write about it or think about it. Ever. Maybe if I kept After from happening, I could keep Mama close somehow.

I tucked deep into the sleeping bag, scared of the darkness just beyond the reach of my light, and brought Robert Frost with me. I read his words out loud, like Mama always did.

And when I come to the garden ground,
The whir of sober birds
Up from the tangle of withered weeds
Is sadder than any words.

Eventually the sound of my lonely voice was worse than the quiet, so I put the book away and shut off the flashlight. As I lay there, wide-awake, I felt the knots of my unwritten words pull even tighter.

For the first time, I worried about getting stuck that way.

5

Zombification

After ten days of trying to talk me into the house, Grandma tossed up her hands and said the word "independent" as though it were a curse word. But Mama always told me I was stubborn as a rusted hinge, so Grandma was no match. She hadn't bothered me yet today, anyway. Maybe she took Sundays off. Besides, I wasn't going anywhere unless it was with Mrs. Greene.

I checked my watch—8:17. Mrs. Greene and Lacey were set to come at nine o'clock. I'd been calling every day and night since I got here just to make sure.

I fished out Mama's cracked eyebrow-plucking mirror and patted my hair. I hadn't washed or brushed it since Mama's funeral. It was a glory of tangles, as Mama would have said. I unzipped her makeup bag and carefully opened her charcoal eye shadow. I touched my finger to the soft powder and rubbed a bit of it under each eye, trying to do it the way Mama had last Halloween when I'd been a zombie.

Next, I took out my biggest pair of jeans and cinched them with a belt. I found a ratty T-shirt Mama had used for sleeping and put it on over my ratty training bra that I'd trained myself right out of at least two months ago. I stood back for the full effect.

I looked awful and I hadn't been eating, and if that wasn't enough to worry Mrs. Greene right into taking me with her, then I'd have to keep going with Plan B—driving Grandma crazy enough that she'd let me go of her own free will.

I practiced my zombie walk, just for good measure.

It was 8:21. Enough time to do another sweep through Mama's room in the house before they got here.

Not wanting Grandma to see me, I tiptoed around the side of the house and hid behind a thick cedar to make sure she was in the garden. I'd been spying since I got here and I'd discovered a few things that, if I were writing in my notebook, I would write in my notebook. Instead, I had to keep it all floating around my mind, which was stressful. Like standing in a room full of bouncing Ping-Pong balls.

1. She didn't sleep. This I'd discovered when I tiptoed into the house the first night to snoop and found her reading by the fire in the living room. She asked me to join her, but I didn't.

Each night after that, I went later and later, but still found her sitting in the same broken-down rocking chair.

2. She barely left the garden, even when it was cold and misty. She was constantly moving things around—trimming, digging, pulling—and she stormed everywhere she went. I wasn't sure if her storming was her way of being sad, a permanent condition, or something brought on by my being here. Considering she'd had twelve years to get used to Mama's being gone, her not wanting me here seemed a whole lot easier to believe.

3. She didn't talk on the phone or have anyone over or go for walks or make lists or pie like a normal grandma. She didn't ask if I brushed my teeth or combed my hair, if I had on clean underwear, or if I'd eaten the trays of food she'd left for me. She didn't ask about Mama, not that I would have told her, or whether or not I liked oatmeal for breakfast, which I didn't.

4. When she was in the house and not in the garden, she played classical music all day, every day. Violins. Piano. Clarinet. Even in her room. It was soft but always there, like a hissing wind.

I left my boots at the door, per Grandma's standing orders, and climbed the stairs to Mama's room to wait for Mrs. Greene and Lacey. The room was empty except for a twin bed, a nightstand, and a dresser. I sat on the bed and looked at the blank walls, the clean floor, and wondered again if this was how Mama had left it or if Grandma had stripped it down years ago, the way a yellow jacket will strip meat from a bone.

Mama's things were stacked neatly in the closet. A whole life's worth of things. White baby shoes and pointe ballet slippers—all that time watching Lacey dance and Mama never mentioned she'd been a dancer too. There was a Girl Scout vest covered in patches, journals filled with sketches, and all sorts of other stuff that told stories I would never know. A porcelain angel with a broken wing. A small jade elephant. Lavender soap.

The sound of a horse neighing came from outside. I jumped up, worrying one of the horses from next door had gotten into Grandma's garden. I didn't think Grandma would take kindly to a garden-munching horse since she worked so hard to keep things perfect. When I got to the window, though, I was surprised to see Grandma at the fence, patting the horse I'd seen my first day, the pretty whitish-gray one with the round belly. Grandma reached in her sweater pocket, pulled out a huge carrot, and fed it to her in chunks. She wiped at her cheeks, and her shoulders shook a little. I wondered if she was crying and tried not to feel bad for her since this whole sorry mess was her fault. She was the one who kicked out her own daughter when she needed a mother most.

As I watched, a girl came to the fence with someone I took to be a small boy following close behind. The girl looked around my age, bundled in a pink jacket and matching scarf. I moved closer to the window to get a better look at the boy, whose entire face was covered in gauze bandages. He wore a Yankees baseball cap. The girl smiled as she talked to Grandma. The boy turned his head and seemed to look right at me. I stepped back from the window, wondering what was wrong with him. If maybe he was burned or had that weird allergy to light.

After a few seconds passed, I looked again. The kids were leading the horse away from the fence. Grandma stood there, hands on her hips, looking up at me as though I'd seen something I shouldn't have.

At twelve minutes after nine, the doorbell rang and I almost tripped as I ran down the stairs. I flung the door open and threw myself into Mrs. Greene's cushy arms. She was dressed in one of her usual crazy-colored shirts and I noticed she'd cut off her long dreads. Lacey dug her head in under our wrapped arms, even though she was usually careful not to mess her hair, so that we became a giant blob of sadness.

"I wanted a new look," Mrs. Greene said, tapping at her tight curls. She had wanted to cut her hair for a long time and Mama had encouraged her, telling her that short hair would show off her beautiful face.

"I like it," I said.

Grandma came down the hallway wiping her hands on a green-checked towel. She took in my zombification but didn't say anything. If Mrs. Greene noticed, she didn't let on either. A spark of panic lit in my belly that this might not work after all.

"It's nice to see you again, Mrs. Greene," Grandma said.

Mrs. Greene wrapped her in a cushy hug, too, and Grandma stiffened before patting her a few times on the back. There was no evidence of crying on Grandma's face. Maybe she'd just gotten dirt in her eyes, or an eyelash. Maybe her shoulders had been trembling because she was cold.

Grandma led us into the living room, where at some point she'd started a fire and put out some crackers, cheese, and an apple cut into pieces. She sat on the edge of a chair. I noticed that she'd changed out of her gardening clothes.

"Well, this is just lovely, Mrs. Jessup," Mrs. Greene

32

said as she looked around the room. She was clearly telling a white lie because the walls were bare and needed a fresh coat of a livelier paint, and the shabby brown sofa sagged in the middle to the point that Mrs. Greene and Lacey were tilted toward each other like the walls of a teepee.

But then I looked past the sofa to the large stone fireplace, where a shiny white wood stove sat gleaming, and to the hardwood beams that went across the high ceilings. I noticed a pretty glass window above the doorway into the hall. The wooden floors were clean and polished. The house was okay, I supposed; it was just Grandma's furniture and walls that needed a makeover.

Grandma fidgeted with one of the blue cloth napkins she'd set out. "I imagine you want to visit with Grace, so I'll just . . ."

"Actually, I'd like to speak with you for a few minutes," Mrs. Greene said. "Go on, Grace, show Lacey around outside."

I tried not to smile, thinking my plan might have worked. Why else would she want to talk to Grandma first?

I pulled Lacey toward the door and caught our reflection in the hallway mirror. My ratted-out hair looked ridiculous against Lacey's perfect ringlets. We were like before and after pictures.

Just outside, I shoved on my worn boots, and then

we walked down the trail arm in arm, Lacey careful to walk over patches of mud in her perfectly clean and new-looking boots.

"Do you think my plan worked?" I said. I'd talked to Lacey every day, and we'd come up with lots of ideas for Plan B, just in case. First I was going to attack Grandma's cleanliness by tracking mud into the house and mixing up her counter and dish sponges. Then I planned on never eating her food, and instead, if I ever got hungry again, sneaking stuff out of the pantry like peanut butter and Marshmallow Fluff. The next part of the plan was "misplacing" things like the can opener and toilet paper. Plus I'd be obnoxious all the time. Lacey thought it was brilliant.

"I hope so," Lacey said. She flipped my knotted hair. "Nice touch. Where are we going?"

"Over there," I said, pointing. "That's the shed."

Lacey's eyes opened wide as she took in the rusted metal roof covered in dead pine needles, the faded green sides and cracked glass window. She looked from the shed to me to the shed again. "Well, if that doesn't make Mom want to take you home today, I don't know what will."

But she didn't sound so sure.

Lacey was pretty in all the ways I wasn't. There were those perfect ringlets, plus she was the shade of brown most people worked for all summer. She complained, though, because it made her feel in between the white of her father and the black of her mother, like she didn't know which side to land on. Not that her father hung around long enough to know what color she'd turn out. We had that in common. She liked to remind me that my father wasn't a deadbeat like hers, and so it was different. But then I'd tell her that her father was still out there, so there was a chance she'd know him someday. We'd agree to disagree on who had it worse until it came up again.

I was jealous of her long-legged, graceful ways after eight years in ballet, because I still managed to fall over my own dumb feet from time to time. When we'd hang out in her room, I'd make her lace up her pointe shoes so I could watch her dance and I'd clap and carry on, since that's what Lacey needed. But more than the pirouettes, I liked the *thunk, thunk, thunk* sound the slippers made as she came down off her toes and waddled across the floor in fits of giggles. She had a great sense of style, too, but fretted that nothing ever looked right. I swear, she'd try on all the clothes she owned, every single morning, often leaving us the option of running all the way to school or being late. It annoyed me that her curls survived intact while mine would frizz somewhere along Whimley Road, so every once in a while I'd suggest that, for heaven's sake, pick your clothes the night before! Until I realized no matter how great she looked, that wasn't what she saw in the mirror, so I'd forgive her until the next time I got too annoyed to keep it to myself.

What I thought about most, though, when I thought about Lacey, was how she liked to write awful poems on purpose so we could laugh about how silly they were, or balance a spoon on her nose and sing "The Star-Spangled Banner." How she was certain I'd be a famous writer one day, and she would be a famous ballerina. Then we would perform together—her dancing, me reading my words— and people would pay us millions of dollars.

No matter how many times I told her that I never in- tended to show all kinds of people my writing, she'd just give me a *pfft* and remind me that I had never intended to talk to Denny Thompson either, but I did.

"That's because you forced me," I'd said.

"Someone had to. Besides, it's not like you're getting married or anything."

She'd twirled around the room singing some kind of crazy song about Denny and his cute earlobes and then flopped onto the bed, fanning herself. "Come on. Just say it. 'I love Denny Thompson.'"

"No," I'd said, arms crossed. But later that night, I wrote it in tiny letters on a smidge of paper and showed it to her. Then we burned it in the fireplace.

Lacey didn't really care if I said things out loud,

wrote them down, or kept them hidden. Being quiet was a part of me, and she liked it just as much as she liked my complimenting her, or my talent for making the perfect bowl of popcorn. Since she was the reason we did things like eat blue lollipops and stick out our tongues at old Mr. Villanueva next door, who'd laugh like he'd been tickled, or climb the tree in the backyard in protest of lima beans, I figured we were a good balance for each other.

"You worry too much," she'd always said, putting her finger right between my eyebrows where I had a permanent crease. Mama said I'd been born pensive, which I had to look up. It meant I was always thinking deeply. Which was true. I liked thinking things through. All the way through from start to finish. Sometimes I even wrote down all the possibilities in these little bubble maps like we learned to do with essays. Doing that made me feel safe from pesky surprises. I figured one of us had to be this way since Mama was always flying off. Since it was just the two of us, that left me.

But along with Mama, Lacey made me see there was more to living than trying to feel safe all the time. Didn't mean I could do it. But I'd tried to think less. To plan less. To just let myself be in the tree protesting lima beans and not thinking about all the ways I might fall out of the tree or how Mama might be upset.

She was the first best friend I'd ever had. There'd never been anyone like her.

Lacey sat down on the flower-garden sofa and looked around. "I knew you were stubborn, Grace. But jeez."

"I'm not being stubborn."

"She said stubbornly," Lacey said, smiling.

I stoked the fire, dumped out water from the bucket, and gave her a *humph*. "It's all part of Plan B."

"Don't you get scared at night?" she said.

"Nope," I lied.

Lacey picked at a thread on the sofa and, when she saw me watching, stopped. "I just don't understand why you can't work your plan from inside the house. You don't have to make yourself miserable too."

"This is torture for Grandma," I said. What I didn't tell her was that I could hear the river from the house sometimes. The hills and valleys made the sound carry in funny ways, though, so I couldn't hear it from the shed at all, even though I could see Grandma's house through the trees.

"I miss you," Lacey said. "It takes me even longer to get dressed in the morning because you're not there to tell me I look okay. I had three tardies in first period just last week."

"I'll be there soon. Your mom knows I'm the only one who can talk sense to you when you're in a snit. And it's going to get worse now that we're almost teenagers." I smiled and poked her arm.

There was a knock on the door and Mrs. Greene came in, the door scraping against the concrete floor. She took in the dish towel curtains I'd hung in the window and the sleeping bag on the flower-garden sofa. "It seems your grandma is not the one forcing you to live in a broken-down shed. That it is you, in fact, who refuses to come in the house."

"I might have exaggerated," I said.

"You flat-out lied, Grace. And what is with your hair? Is that makeup under your eyes?"

She came at me with her thumbs and wiped away the eye shadow. Then she nudged herself right between me and Lacey. "We had a deal," she said to me.

"I'm trying."

"Trying to give your poor grandmother a stroke."

"I just want to come back to your house."

Mrs. Greene gave me a fierce hug. "We will always be here for you, but this is your home now."

I mumbled into her shirt, "You aren't taking me with you."

She took me by the shoulders. "I would never leave you in a bad place. Can you believe that?"

I looked into Mrs. Greene's face, trying hard not to believe her. Trying hard to ignore all the days of living in her house, where she never once lied or took advantage or did anything untrustworthy. I'd watched her put change into donation cans and wrap blankets around homeless people and take in more strays—dogs, cats, people—than she should have. Including me and Mama. She reminded me of a thousand-year-old tree. Her roots went down and her arms went out and there was no knocking her over with anything less than a bulldozer.

"But Mama didn't want this place to be home or we would have come back. There was a good reason Mama stayed away."

"I'm sure she had reasons. But don't you think you need to decide for yourself if they were good ones?"

I pulled away and chewed my thumbnail.

"Your grandmother tells me you haven't been eating either," Mrs. Greene said.

There it was, the moment I'd been waiting for. She wouldn't just leave me here to starve to death.

"No. I haven't been hungry." I tried to look especially pathetic. "Grandma is a terrible cook."

Lacey nodded. "Look at her, Mom. She's dropped five pounds at least. And she was skinny to begin with."

Mrs. Greene heaved a big sigh. "I hate doing this. But you don't seem to be adjusting well, so we're all going to take a break."

"What?" Lacey and I both said together.

"Your grandma and I decided you and Lacey could talk on Saturdays, but not during the school week. We aren't coming back to visit for a couple of months."

"But . . . !" I said, words failing. Lacey just looked down at her hands.

"You have to give yourself a chance here. And hanging on to us isn't the way to do it," Mrs. Greene said.

It felt like the last little thread connecting me to anything familiar and loved snapped and I was falling and falling down some bottomless hole. It was hard to catch my breath.

It must have showed in my face, because Mrs. Greene said, "If you need help, Grace, you have to ask for it. I know you don't want to talk about what happened, but—"

"It's fine. I'll be fine."

Mrs. Greene didn't push and instead tried talking to me about my first day of school tomorrow and how she believed in me. How much fun Lacey and I would have writing letters to each other since Grandma didn't have a computer and wouldn't get me an e-mail account anyway. Mrs. Greene wanted me to send her poems, and I didn't tell her how I wasn't going to be writing, that somehow not writing was going to keep Mama close. It was the kind of thing I could have told her Before, but instead, I just kept my arms crossed tight and my mouth closed. Lacey still stared at her hands.

"Well, aren't you two a pair. Come on, then." Mrs. Greene stood up.

She took my hands and helped me off the sofa. Then she kissed my forehead. I put my arms around her and held on tight, wondering how I'd ever let go. Lacey wedged herself in.

"This isn't forever, Grace. Just for a little while," Mrs. Greene said.

Lacey hugged me tight, and then I watched them drive away.

6

Twin Hearts

In my dream, Mama sat on a wide, flat rock in the middle of the river. It was nightfall, and the deep green of the water moved in slow motion beneath her feet. There were two sandhill cranes, one on each side of her, like guardians. Mama stood and smiled, arms outstretched. I wasn't surprised to see she matched the cranes with her own set of wings spread wide. My heart swelled at seeing her again. I had so much to tell her.

I walked into the water, braving the cold and the pointy rocks.

The cranes startled and flew off, frightened by my clumsy splashing. Then, as though they knew the way and she didn't, Mama flapped her own great wings and flew off after them, giving one last sorrowful look over her shoulder, blond hair streaming behind in soft waves. I woke with the effort of trying to call her back.

I didn't have much time to gather myself before the *crunch, crunch, crunch* of gravel outside let me know

Grandma was coming. I listened to see if her footsteps went toward the mailbox or the shed.

Darn it.

Grandma walked in wearing her usual oversized brown cardigan and overalls, plus knee pads covered in dirt from the garden. A bandana held back the hair from her forehead, all of it twisted into a tight bun at her neck. She stared me down with blue eyes, so much like mine and Mama's, as she set a big red bag on the sofa. From the bag, she took out a pretty purple sweater, jeans, and brand-new Converse.

"I picked up a few things the last time I was in Nevada City. I wasn't sure what you'd need," she said, matter-of-fact. "We can shop for more if you'd like."

"Do you think Mama didn't provide for me? Is that what you're saying?"

Grandma squinted like some part of me had gone out of focus. She ignored my question and stared around the room, like Mrs. Greene did the day before, taking in the old rag rug I'd shaken out and set on the floor, the stack of boxes I'd taken out of Mama's room. She lifted a box flap. The one with the pointe ballet shoes and the Girl Scout vest.

It wasn't a compulsion—to gather every bit of Mama that I could. Every broken necklace and pair of stockings.

Mary Lou Jenkins from my second-grade class in But-
tonwillow, who used to pull out one hair at a time and eat
it like spaghetti? That was a compulsion. This was just a
strong need. A water-sunshine-sleep kind of need.

Grandma took the ballet shoes out of the box. "These
are mine."

I blinked in surprise. I'd already created a space in my
mind for Mama's dancing. I couldn't at all wrap my head
around this new information. Grandma, with her gardening knee pads and lumberjack coat, had been a ballerina.

"There's a lot you don't know." She set the slippers
back in the box and closed the lid. She touched the cross
at her neck. "We've got to start somewhere, Grace. I want
you to come in the house."

"I do come in the house. I have to use your bathroom,
don't I?"

Grandma looked at the boxes again. Then she turned
and walked outside. When she came back, she carried a
banged-up metal toolbox. It looked just like one Mama
had.

She sat on the couch and set the toolbox beside her.
"Your mama used to make birds out of metal and found
objects."

"Don't you think I know that?"

"So she kept making them." It wasn't a question.

"Of course she did."

She patted the sofa as if I should sit. "Do you have any of her birds?"

"No," I said, suddenly hopeful. "Do you?"

"Open the toolbox."

I sat down beside it, carefully opening the rusted blue lid, and found a tray of what Mama called her delicates. Random letters from a Scrabble board, miniature brass numbers and letters, fortunes from fortune cookies, Monopoly game pieces.

Hands shaking, I took out the tray and set it on my lap. The space underneath was full of bird parts. At least that was what I saw in the bent-up pieces of metal, broken watches, and spoons.

Mixed in with all that was a small half-finished bird. Tears burned my eyes, but I wouldn't let them fall in front of Grandma.

"Go ahead," she said. "Take a look."

I lifted the bird out. The rivets hadn't been closed around the bottom, and there weren't any wings or head. But I could tell from the long, graceful neck and legs that it was meant to be a crane.

Grandma fussed with Mama's quilt, folding it this way and that, and I thought about Mama's treasure hunts, how they always started with a crane. While Grandma was folding, I held my breath and tilted the unfinished bird the tiniest bit so I could see inside the dark opening of the body. The opening wasn't very wide, almost paper thin. But I could see the edge of something just inside, something I'd have to pry out. I couldn't help it and let out a small sound.

"What is it?" Grandma asked.

"Nothing."

I stared at that little bird and wondered if this was the start of a new treasure hunt, if it was an honest-to-goodness sign from Mama. The hope sat awkwardly in my chest, beating there like a twin heart.

"You can keep the box, but you'll have to give me something in return. Take meals in the house. Help with chores when I ask," Grandma said.

I thought it over. It was fair, I supposed. "Fine."

Grandma stood up and stretched, then headed for the door and pulled it open. "Well, what are you waiting for?"

"You mean, right now?"

"Breakfast is ready. Grab your clothes." She nodded toward the toolbox. "It'll be here when you get back."

"Will it?"

Grandma put her hands on her hips. "I guess a toolbox-stealing thief might find his way in here before you get home from school. But it's entirely unlikely."

I wasn't taking any chances that a Grandma-sized thief might go back on her word, so I carefully packed the crane in a T-shirt and slipped it inside my backpack. I grabbed clothes and my latest notebook.

Even though I had no intention of writing, leaving it behind would have felt like leaving a piece of my own self behind. A necessary piece, like an elbow for leaning. I figured I needed all the elbows I could get today.

7

Grilled
Cheese

Grandma went out to warm the truck, but it wouldn't start, so she came back inside and called Sheriff Bergum. Why you needed a sheriff to start your truck, I would never know.

I hoped I could stay out of school one more day, really check out the inside of the unfinished crane in the privacy of my own shed, but those hopes were crushed a few minutes later when the sheriff's car pulled into the driveway. He must have been close. But then again, everywhere in this town was close.

I tried to think straight about the unfinished bird. It was in an old toolbox that Mama left behind years ago. She couldn't have possibly meant for me to find what was inside. But what if she had? I could just see her setting up a treasure hunt for her baby to follow one day before she knew she'd be leaving, before her whole life turned into one big search for home.

As much as my rational mind tried to talk me into

facts, it didn't have as much power as my imagination and the feeling that Mama was so close, I could almost smell the peeled-apple scent of her soap.

Whatever was going on, it would have to wait until after school. In the meantime, I finished getting ready in the downstairs bathroom, taking handfuls of water to sponge down my poky hair until the frizz was sort of under control. I took Grandma's new clothes, which she'd picked up on our way out of the shed, and tucked them behind the toilet.

The horn blared as I buttoned Mama's coat over my own jeans and sweatshirt. I double-checked my backpack for bird, binder and pencils, and my map of California. Every place we'd ever lived was pinpricked on that map, and it gave me a solid feeling on the inside to have it with me. My notebook was there, nestled in beside my binder. I might not have been able to write in it, but at least it was where it was supposed to be.

Like arms and legs and hair and nose, everything was all in its proper place. It was my insides that needed an inventory. I was certain if they ran my body through one of those X-ray machines, they'd find stuff missing. I didn't know what exactly. Not my heart, because I could feel it there, beating on as though nothing had happened. But maybe some deep-down place that knew how to love and smile and feel light as feathers on sunshiny days. That part was clean gone.

The horn blared again and I wanted to punch something. Instead, I looked in the mirror and repeated the words Mama would have me say each time I started a new school.

"You can do this. You are brave and wise. You are loved."

I felt her hands running through my hair, taming it in all the ways I couldn't. There were so many things I should have paid attention to.

I slung my backpack over one shoulder and walked onto the porch. Sheriff Bergum was parked right next to the open hood of Grandma's truck. Grandma didn't have a name for her Chevy, so I'd taken to calling her Granny Smith in my own mind because she was the exact color of a Granny Smith apple. The sheriff himself stood over the open engine with a look of determination, as though he wasn't used to anything getting the best of him. As I approached the truck, he looked up and smiled at me, running a thick-fingered hand over his bald head.

I'd heard the term *barrel-chested* in books but always thought it was an impossible description of a person. Like *sharp-nosed* or *whip-thin*. Something fit for a cartoon character. But Sheriff Bergum actually looked like if he unpeeled his shirt, I might just see the ribs of a barrel in there. He was wide everywhere else, and tall, and I imagined criminals made sure to commit their crimes in other counties. All that bigness was almost scary like a storm coming, or a really big wave, but he was handsome, too, in a rugged, stubbled sort of way. The kind of handsome some of the ladies around here might stick their cats up a tree for, just so they could call for help.

"It still won't start," Grandma said as I dropped my backpack on the seat next to a small bag of gardening tools. I didn't climb in and if she noticed my lack of purple sweater and new Converse, she didn't comment.

"Then why are you blaring your horn at me?"

"So we can leave as soon as this truck starts," Grandma said like I was a ninny.

"Try it again," Sheriff Bergum called in a voice deep as roots.

Grandma twisted the key, the truck sending unnatural sounds out into the morning.

"I can give you a ride in," Sheriff Bergum said, wiping his hands on a greasy towel. He bent over to rest his arms on Grandma's open window.

I narrowed my eyes. No one on this earth did things for free, and that was a proven fact. Just take our old landlord, Johnny B. He gave us room and board in his cheap motel for half the price, Mama thinking she would clean rooms and cook meals to make up the difference. But Johnny B. had more in mind than Mr. Clean and a pot roast dinner, which prompted move number six. I'd learned that with some people the truth was a hard thing to pin down, as it was usually hidden in the deep valleys between their words.

Besides, no way was I riding in the back of a police car on my first day of school. No way was I letting anyone drive Daisy either.

"You need to give her a name," I said.

"Give who a name?" Grandma said.

"The truck. We had a name for our car and Mama talked real nice to her, like with plants. That car always started right up."

"You want me to talk to the truck?" Grandma said real quiet, like it was occurring to her I might have slipped clear off my nut.

Sheriff Bergum looked amused. "Come on, Miranda. Give it a try."

"I most certainly will not."

Just to poke at her, I ran my hand along the crisp green metal. "There you go, Granny Smith. You take your time. I know you can do it."

When I walked to the tailgate, Grandma stared at me through the rearview mirror; her eyes were almost kind.

"You can try it again," I said.

In a shuddering cough of smelly gray smoke, the truck started right up. Even I was surprised.

"Well, now. That is impressive. We should send you out on service calls with Old Mac. He could use you instead of a battery charger," Sheriff Bergum said.

"I'll make an appointment with Mac today. Thank you for coming, Pete."

"How could I resist your charms?" he said with a wink. "You're still late, though. It appears I'll have to give you an escort." He said it with a wink to me, as though I were a seven-year-old boy who had waited my entire seven-year-old-boy life for something like that.

Sheriff Bergum set his lights to whirling, but Grandma wouldn't go past twenty-five miles per hour. We were the slowest-moving police escort in the history of police escorts. I almost asked her why in the heck she drove so slow, but then it occurred to me she'd lost her husband in a car accident, so I kept my mouth shut.

I slid down as far as I could, eyeballs looking over the bottom edge of the window. As we came out on Ridge Road, the stormy-sky horse from next door was standing at the wooden fence. She nodded her head as we passed.

"It would be easier to talk to Lacey if I had an e-mail account," I said for the hundredth time.

"When I was your age, we wrote letters. It's a lost art."

"So I guess a cell phone is out?" Mama and I had never had cell phones as they were too expensive. I'd been hopeful, though, that I might be able to guilt Grandma into one. Then maybe Lacey and I could sneak in conversations whenever we wanted.

"There's no reception in the mountains."

As though it wasn't bad enough I had to live with Grandma, I had to live with Grandma stuck back in time.

"You know," Grandma said, "I was wondering if you've seen my spatula or the can opener. I went to use both this morning and they aren't in their usual place. Maybe you put them in the wrong drawer."

"Maybe."

I had to turn all the way to the window to hide my smile. And then I felt bad. I was committed to Plan B, but she had just given me the toolbox, after all.

I counted trees out the window. When I hit thirty-seven Grandma said, "So what did you and your mom name your car?"

I contemplated not telling her, but a tiny break from Plan B wouldn't hurt anything.

"Daisy," I said.

She nodded as though that made perfect sense.

The church and the school shared a parking lot, and Grandma pulled into the same space she used for the funeral, waving the sheriff off. There were a million empty spaces between the school and us.

"No one dings the doors this way," Grandma declared.

As Sheriff Bergum drove by, he put two fingers to his eyes and then pointed at me. He'd be watching. Then he winked again and drove off.

Grandma clutched her black purse and got out.

I stared forward for a few seconds and took a deep breath, asking Mama for help to get through my day, even though I was pretty much an old pro at first days. As I said my last few words, I noticed something shiny caught in the bushes.

Grandma opened my door. "Good heavens, do I need a crowbar to get you out?"

"I need a minute. To myself."

"Don't be long," Grandma said, and hurried toward the office. She hadn't even bothered to take off her knee pads.

I got out of the truck and watched Grandma until she was out of sight, then turned back to the bushes. They were hedge-like, thick with leaves and white buds, gardenias thinking about blooming. I reached toward the silvery paper, trying hard not to catch the sharp twig-thin branches with my arm. It didn't work. I drew blood on the back of my hand before I got to whatever it was stuck deep in the bush. I pulled it out as carefully as I could and got two more scratches for my trouble.

It was an origami crane, dirty and weathered.

I stared at that little bird, blinked, and stared again. I

almost wished Grandma was here so I could make sure she was seeing what I was seeing. The breeze picked up and the bird shuddered in my hand like it was pondering the best way to take off.

Mama thought birds were signposts sent to let us know we were headed in the right direction. We'd look for birds on road signs, in murals or billboards, anywhere they might show up. So I took that bird as a sign of encouragement.

Whatever doubts I'd had that Mama might be trying to tell me something were gone.

There was a steady drizzle as I set off across the asphalt toward Lincoln School. I pocketed the crane into Mama's peacoat and tried not to let the hope run away with me. But it made perfect sense. Mama had always said she'd never leave me, that not even death could separate us. Late into the night, when she couldn't sleep and she'd climb into bed with me to read Robert Frost, she'd whisper that she'd always be there, falling with the raindrops, turning herself to birdsong, warming the top of my head on a hot summer day. Then she'd laugh and say my poems were rubbing off on her.

Because Mama didn't leave a last will and testament or any other sort of directions as to what she wanted, she must be trying to let me know—in our own secret way— that she wanted me to follow the treasure-hunt clues.

That they would tell me where I belonged. Which I already knew was with Mrs. Greene.

A chill ran along my shoulders at the idea that Mama was still there, really and truly there. A little voice whispered that I was crazy. But then I heard Mama's voice, strong and true. *Don't think so much, Grace.*

"Let go of my hand!"

A smallish girl with pixie-cut brown hair dragged an even smaller boy right toward me on the sidewalk, fast, and scattered my Mama thoughts. At the last second, she saw me frozen there and jerked to the left. Two books, a rolling red suitcase, and the boy went tripping onto the grass.

"I'm sorry!" she called over her shoulder as she ran past. "I'll be right back!"

I turned to watch her head into the school parking lot, waving her arms like a lunatic.

"She's trying to catch my mom before she leaves," a voice said from the grass. The boy reached his hand out to me, both hands wrapped in bandages.

"I'm Maximilian Patrick Brannigan. That was Johanna. I'm sorry she almost fell on you."

He was seven, eight tops, with hair so wispy, it looked more like a halo than something you could tug on with a brush. He picked his Yankees baseball cap off the grass and shoved it on his head.

"You have the horses next door," I said.

"Yep."

A few papers blew across the lawn out of an open textbook. Max stomped on them rather than let them get away, and I helped as best I could. Science notes. Math scribbles. He had a hard time picking up paper with his thumb and bandaged fingers.

"Jo's going to be mad her notes got dirty," he said.

"*She's* going to be mad?"

"She won't be mad at us. She'll be mad at herself."

As I chased after one last sheet of paper, Jo ran back into view holding a brown paper lunch sack. She wore an oversized orange sweater, black leggings that hugged her skinny legs, and combat boots. I noticed her hair was exactly the same as Max's, squirrel brown and wispy. She had a toothy smile. They were like two of those little Russian dolls that fit one inside the other.

A new white truck drove by slowly, holding up a line of cars, BRANNIGAN & SON CONSTRUCTION printed on the front door panel. The window cranked down and a woman with Jo's turned-up nose called out, "Eat every last bit of that lunch, Max Brannigan!" and then with a wave she was gone.

I was embarrassed for Max, but none of the kids walking up the path seemed to notice.

"Try and remember next time," Jo said, handing Max

the lunch sack. Then she turned to me. "I'm so sorry, Grace. Are you all right? Of course you're all right. Look at you. You're good. You're fine. Well, maybe not fine, but not hurt. And that's good."

Jo grabbed a handful of papers and shoved them into her backpack. "Look at my notes! There are grass stains and smudgy footprint stains, and now maybe I'll read a word in my notes as *exothermic* when it's really *endothermic* and I'll flunk my science quiz."

"You don't have to do everything for me. It's not like I'm an imbecile," Max said.

"You mean *invalid*."

"Whatever."

"Fine."

"Fine!"

Max grabbed the handle of the suitcase and turned toward me. "It was nice to meet you, Grace." He flashed me a missing-toothed smile and stuck his tongue out at Jo. Then he stormed off, suitcase bumping behind, clutching his lunch sack. For a second, it felt like I'd always been there, stuck right between them like grilled cheese.

Jo reached into her backpack and pulled out a brush, brushing frantically at her short hair until it was shiny and electrified. She stopped as suddenly as she started.

"You must think we're crazy," she said.

"I've known crazier."

"Well, that's a comfort. Come on, your grandma went inside. She asked me to show you around today, so we'll start with the office."

I followed her into the building and down a long hallway. The tiled floor reflected the lights from above.

"I'm Jo, by the way. I wanted to come by and introduce myself before, but your grandma said . . . ," she trailed off.

That I'd moved myself into her shed like a crazy person? That she wished I'd never come to live with her? "It's okay," I said.

We stopped in front of the glass office door and I saw Grandma filling out paperwork. She touched a pencil to the tip of her tongue.

It was a dead-end moment, the perfect time for Jo to scurry off. Instead, she looked me straight in the eye. "Your grandma isn't one for big emotions, in case you haven't figured that out. But she's glad you're here."

I didn't know what to say to that.

The bell rang, and Grandma came out of the office. She put her hand on Jo's shoulder. "I see you've met Grace."

Seeing her hand there filled me with all kinds of confusing feelings, anger, curiosity . . . jealousy? Those feelings made me want to run away. I touched the crane in my pocket.

The run-away feeling didn't go away as I followed Jo to my first-period class.

8

Refolding
a Map

When I walked into third-period art, the teacher, Mrs. Snickels, reached out and shook my hand. She was tall and angular, all squares and triangles, like the Picasso paintings from our yard-sale art book. Even her black hair was cut in a sharp wedge. The collection of her reminded me of Mama's birds, somehow. How there was always more to them than just rivets and glue and metal.

Everyone still had on their name tags from first-period English. Mr. Flinch, who was the principal as well as the English and social studies teacher, had insisted they wear them since it was my first day of school. All eighteen seventh-graders—probably glued together by PTA moms and Flat Stanley projects since kindergarten—were like one big family, or so it seemed. And Mrs. Julian had done her best to welcome me into it with a giant bear hug and a small basket of cookies in pre-algebra. Right before she slammed her giant book of sudoku on

Stubbie's desk after he blew a spit wad at a girl named Beth Crinkle.

There was Ginger Peppers, who was so expressive, she could have been mistaken for a mime if she didn't talk so much. She had straight peanut-colored hair that looked almost long enough for her to sit on, and a habit of swinging it to one side or the other for emphasis. Beth Crinkle's name tag had been written with a label maker. She told me twice that her mother owned an inspirational T-shirt business and that she helped with the slogans, which she showed me. Her T-shirt read IT TAKES A VILLAGE. She liked lists. They were written all over her notebook and binder. *Seven Things I Hate about Mornings* and *Fifty-Three Things That Make Me Happy to Be Me*. She drew hearts in every other square inch of space, of which there wasn't much.

There was spit-wad Stubbie, and Archer Lee Hamilton, whose name tag actually read ARCHER LEE HAMILTON like he was practicing to be president or something.

Jo sat alone at a tall table, fidgeting with the settings on a movie camera, and patted the seat next to her. Stubbie nudged Archer as I walked past, and Archer gave me a cheesy grin he might have meant to be something else. Maybe a flirty grin? A welcoming smile? Like how you sit down to draw a duck, only it ends up looking more like a caterpillar, and so you just go with it.

My brain was overloaded, the new names and classroom numbers floating around like bits of confetti. Even though there were only eighteen names and six classes, they tacked themselves to long lists of other names and classes from other schools so that I kept forgetting where I was. I sat next to Jo and out of habit, I reached for my notebook so I could write down words and relieve some first-day-of-school pressure. Then I remembered why I couldn't do that and bit my nails instead.

"Mrs. Snickels asked me to fill you in on the final project," Jo said. "It's due at the end of the year, so you have about eight more weeks. There isn't much of a theme; she just wants you to choose something you love or feel passionate about. Her only rule is that the passion has to come through in the project somehow. You can use any medium—photography, art, collage. Last year, someone did a series of photos of a garden as it bloomed. I'm doing a documentary. Just make sure you check with Mrs. Snickels to see if your project is okay."

That all sounded manageable, only I didn't plan on being there in June.

"Here." She slid a small stack of stapled pages toward me. She whispered, "I've known most everyone since kindergarten, some before. I figured I'd write down some basic information to fill you in."

The first page said *Things to Know* at the top. I couldn't decide if it was sweet or creepy. "Thanks."

"Don't mention it."

There were eighteen wooden box frames along one side of the wall with names underneath. Each frame held an object of some kind: an engraved stone that said PEACE (Beth), a Playbill from the musical *Wicked* (Ginger), a Barbie-sized director's chair (Jo). In the bottom corner was an empty frame with my name beneath it.

"What goes in the box?" I asked Jo.

"Whatever you feel like sharing."

"What if you don't feel like sharing anything?"

"It happens. Stubbie protested just before Thanksgiving. He said he was exerting his right to privacy under the Constitution. Mrs. Snickels said it was a perfect example of how nothing can mean something in art."

Mrs. Snickels tinkled a bell to get our attention. "We're going to start something new today. Self-portraits."

She dug through the piles of paper on her desk and came up with a drawing she clipped to the whiteboard. It was a pencil-sketched self-portrait of half her face. She had drawn her short black hair, funny dark-rimmed glasses, and a crooked smile. I liked it. She didn't make herself look like something she wasn't.

She picked up a bag from her desk and handed out mirrors.

"The self-portrait should take up only half the page—which half is up to you. The other half is a surprise that we will finish in a few weeks.

"Try and keep in mind that some of it will come from the mirror, but some of it should come in the form of expression so that the inside of you is on the page too. Chiaroscuro! The transition between light and dark. Show me what you've learned about contour."

When she was done handing out the mirrors, she went back to her desk and banged a gong.

"It's a meditation thing," Jo whispered.

I shrugged. I'd seen weirder things from teachers. Like Mr. Langston, who had to touch his nose, his pencil holder, and the top of his head before he could get up from his chair.

Mrs. Snickels brought me a book on portraiture. "We've already done some work with faces this year. Take your time looking through the exercises in the book and if you have any questions, let me know."

I flipped through a few pages and studied some of the techniques. Then I looked at myself in the silver-backed mirror, deciding to start with my hair and the shape of my face. But as I touched the pencil to paper, all I wanted was to write down words in my notebook. I took a deep breath and thought them instead.

If only my words
could build a path
to where you are.

I felt a little better after that, and so the sketching came easier. I went through the motions, letting my hand and arm do the work and leaving my brain out of it, and eventually the bell rang.

As we rolled our portraits into tubes, Jo snuck a look. "You're good at faces," she said.

I shrugged. My hand knew where to put the shading of a cheekbone, the curve of a brow. I could be one of those people who drew portraits in carnivals, maybe. It wasn't art like Mama's.

But I had to admit there was a certain satisfaction in drawing something true, even if it was the sad eye of a girl I didn't recognize.

Everyone was eating inside the cafetorium—half cafeteria, half auditorium—with its giant banner proclaiming TRAVEL THE WORLD, ONE BOOK AT A TIME! It had sprinkled earlier, so I took a wad of paper towels from the girls' room and wiped down a place to sit outside under the awning. I dumped out the lunch I'd packed, which consisted of a peanut butter sandwich with the crusts cut off and a Ding Dong, not that I was hungry.

Making sure no one was watching, I pulled my backpack onto the bench beside me and unzipped it. I set the T-shirt on my lap and unwrapped the bird I'd found in the toolbox, looking again into the sliver of an opening, reassured by that little edge of paper inside.

Part of me wished Mama could just leave me an honest-to-goodness sign, like a poster in front of the school that said *Let this sign hereby notify the powers that be that Gracie May Jessup should be living with Mrs. Greene in Hood, California, not her grandmother.*

Jo walked toward me from the cafetorium, her short hair blowing in the wind, and I quickly wrapped the bird in the T-shirt. "Come and sit with us. It's cold out here."

I looked past her to the table inside filled with girls all babbling at one another. Ginger was laughing and flapping her arms like a chicken. Archer and Stubbie sat at the other end of the same table, where apparently Stubbie wasn't done with his spit-wad tricks. A sour-looking woman in a hairnet and a frilly white apron walked up and took the straw right out of his mouth. Archer laugh-snorted his milk all over the table and immediately began mopping it up with whatever napkins were handy.

"Thanks, but I kind of wanted the fresh air. It smells like melted plastic in there," I said.

Jo wiped a space across from me with the arm of her jacket and sat down. She swung the end of her long, pink scarf over one shoulder. There was a spit wad in her hair. "We've all tried guessing at that smell. Beth thinks Mr. Joe is boiling his mops before school every day to sanitize them. He's a germaphobe. And if anyone understands germaphobes, it's Beth."

"You have a spit wad in your hair," I said.

She shook her head and it went flying off. "Thanks."

I tried to eat my sandwich. Cardboard.

"That's Mrs. Donatello," she said, nodding toward Hairnet Lady. "She yells in Italian because she thinks we can't understand what she's saying. But Beth wrote down a few words one time and we looked up the translation." She waggled her eyebrows. "Now we all know how to swear in Italian."

Mrs. Donatello hurried away from Archer and Stubbie, all flailing arms, to deal with one of the smaller kids, who'd dropped his whole lunch tray and burst into tears. Stubbie immediately grabbed for another straw.

"I was wondering if you had a chance to look over my list." She took a big bite of the hot dog she'd brought with her. Then she said around a mouthful, "Hom hahs ah sah guh."

"You shouldn't eat those, you know. They put cow hooves in hot dogs," I said.

She squeezed an extra packet of ketchup on the hot dog, then took another big bite. "There, now I don't taste the cow's hoof you just put in my mind."

I took the list out of my backpack to make her happy, and handed it to her. She tucked a piece of hair behind her ear.

"We should start with number seven, Archer Lee Hamilton, since he can't keep his eyes off you," she said.

I about choked, even though I wasn't eating anything. The last thing I could imagine right now was dealing with boy feelings.

She took a swig of milk and cleared her throat. "When we were six, Archer decided to dig in the side yard for hamsters. He kept insisting if he dug a hole deep enough, he'd find one. By the end of the week, he had most of us helping him until Ms. Pimkin discovered us and put a stop to it.

"When we got to school the next Monday, we had a hamster for a class pet. Ms. Pimkin had been very impressed with our determination. Everyone cheered for Archer. And since he was pretty clumsy and his pants never matched his shirts, his hero status was short-lived. Until he turned eleven and grew six inches and some pretty decent muscles."

I looked over her list and found Archer Lee Hamilton

and the story she'd just told. I found Beth Crinkle, who took a label maker with her everywhere and was furious with her brown curly hair because it was impossible to organize, which I sympathized with. Then there was Ginger, who was known to break out into Shakespearean monologues, which Jo was starting to think she made up as she went along, because who would know the difference? Stubbie had just tried to do a stand-up routine for the talent show, frozen there like a side of beef, and had to be walked offstage. It went on and on.

"When did you write all this?"

She shrugged. "Over the weekend. Since we didn't get a chance to talk or anything. Feel free to ask questions. Choosing the right details gives me good practice since I'm doing a documentary for my final art project. In fact, I should interview you. You probably know more than I do, and I've lived here all my life."

"Know more about what?"

"Your grandma, and Bear River Park."

"Sorry, but I don't know anything about either."

If she thought that was surprising, she didn't show it. She ate the last bite of hot dog. "I haven't done all my research, but your grandma designed Bear River Park fifteen years ago. Everyone has a story about it. Beth Crinkle was born there. Her parents were listening to a Barry Manilow cover band at the gazebo, and apparently her mom boogied down a little too hard to 'Copacabana' and her water broke. Your grandma designed a lot of things in town. Gardens and stuff."

It was strange how each new thing about Grandma stretched the picture of her I'd been carrying around in my mind. It took effort to squeeze her back down to the right size and shape. Like refolding a map.

"What's your documentary about?"

She put a finger to her chin. "Well, it's mostly about the park and how important it is to our town. I don't know. I haven't edited it yet. I'm still looking for my theme. There's a short film competition I'm entering too."

She looked so excited I almost wanted to touch her arm to see if it might shock me like static electricity. Then maybe I could feel something.

"I want to go to film school. How about you?"

"Um . . ."

Beth and Ginger came outside giggling, and saved me from having to answer. Ginger was projecting, as though trying to be heard by teachers on the other side of the school. "Rather long this winded jester takes to fix his shrunken pride!" Stubbie blew a spit wad toward their backs, but it fell short of the open doorway. He looked around to see if he'd been caught, but Mrs. Donatello was at the other end of the room.

Jo gathered her trash. "On cold days like this, we go to

the library for the rest of lunch. It doesn't smell like boiled mops in there. Mrs. Hall always has stuff for us to do."

"Sometimes it's even fun," Beth said. "Like the time we got to reorganize the picture books and label them!"

Jo and Ginger looked at her and then burst out laughing.

"What?" Beth said. "Organization is the cornerstone of life. When I have my own advice column, every Monday will be Organization Day. What better way to start the week?"

"Technically, Sunday is the first day of the week," Jo said.

Beth rolled her eyes. "Do you always have to be so specific?"

"Um, yeah," Jo said. "Do you always have to point out when I'm being specific?"

"Maybe next time," I said.

Jo and Beth glared at each other for a minute, and Beth linked arms with Ginger. "See you later, then," she said to me, and they walked off together.

"Listen," I said as Jo stood up. "This is my fourteenth new school. You don't have to be nice to me. I can manage. I always have."

"I'm not being nice because someone told me to. I actually am nice. Plus I thought you could use a friend."

"I have friends," I said with more gusto than I should have.

"After fourteen schools, I should hope so."

I blinked a few times while she dumped her garbage in the can. "You know, I'll never be able to look at another hot dog without thinking of you. That wouldn't sound so weird if you knew me better."

If I was lucky, I wouldn't be here long enough to figure it out one way or another.

9

A Postcard
from Heaven

As soon as I got back from school, I made a dash
for the shed and started collecting tools. A thin metal nail
file from Mama's makeup kit and her eyebrow tweezers.
I also went through Grandpa's doodads at the back of the
shed, but none of the screwdrivers or wood files looked
thin enough. I grabbed them anyway in case I had to pry
the bird open a tiny bit. Then I dumped a bunch of nuts
and bolts out of a jar with the word KERR on it.

I sat on the flower-garden sofa and used the nail file to
carefully poke inside the bird. It took a while, but I finally
got a corner of thick paper out. Then I used the tweezers
to pull the rest free.

It was an old postcard folded into a square. I wiped
sweaty palms on my jeans and then unfolded it.

The postcard showed a section of storefronts on Main
Street. Threads was the store in the center of the photo.
I thought about the woman in the muumuu and cowboy
hat from Mama's funeral, who'd introduced herself as

Margery. She'd told me to come talk to her, but I'd for-gotten all about it. I turned the postcard over, and written in blue ink was the phrase *A Secret Meadow*. Something about the idea of a secret meadow seemed familiar, but I had no idea why.

I unscrewed the lid of the Kerr jar and put the postcard inside. I took the origami out of my pocket and set it be-side the postcard, staring at them both through the glass. It might have been my imagination, but I could almost swear they had a kind of glow.

I put everything away and wrote a letter to Lacey, fill-ing her in about the unfinished bird from Mama's toolbox and the origami I'd found as a signpost. I told her about the postcard and Margery's store in town, how Mama must have set a new treasure hunt for me to follow, her way of leading me home, just the way she always did. And home was Mrs. Greene's house.

I knew it sounded crazy, but Lacey would believe me. That's what best friends did.

I decided to wait until after my phone call with Lacey on Saturday to go to Threads. Hopefully, she'd get my letter by then and have good advice. Plus I needed a day when I had enough time to ride my bike into town, figure out the next clue, and get back, all without Grandma knowing.

In the meantime, my mission to do more Plan B

sabotage was stopped in its tracks by Grandma's insomnia. After a couple nights of sneaking out later and later, I was starting to wonder if Grandma went to sleep at all, or if she was having trouble, like me.

I'd thought about calling off Plan B now that there was a treasure hunt to follow, but it was satisfying in this deep-down way to try and drive Grandma crazy.

I decided to set my watch alarm just in case I fell asleep, which was a good thing because I slept for almost an hour. When I woke to the beeping, my hair was sweaty and my throat hurt. There'd been a dog in my Mama dream this time, a big German shepherd, the tip of his leash dangling in the water. When he barked, the white mist of his breath had grown and grown until I couldn't see Mama out on the rock anymore. Every time I tried to wade into the water after her, the dog blocked my way, baring his teeth.

I shivered in the sleeping bag, feeling the chill of the river, and wondered if my dreams were bringing me one piece of Mama's death at a time, so that eventually I'd be able to see the whole thing without wanting to throw up. I turned on my flashlight. It was three o'clock in the morning. Grandma had to be sleeping by now.

I stoked the embers in the stove and added wood so it would be warmer when I got back. Then I shoved on my boots and walked out into the moonless night, dragging my feet through the mud, the light from Grandma's porch leading the way. The rest of the downstairs lights were off.

I didn't take off my muddy boots as I went inside and tracked the mud from one light to the next, unscrewing bulbs so she might think they were out, and poured her liquid laundry detergent down the sink, replacing it with dishwashing soap. I'd washed laundry with dishwashing soap once and we'd almost drowned in bubbles.

By the time I was done, the floor was a mess of mud and another mess was about to happen the next time she did laundry, which I figured was enough for one night.

As I tiptoed through the hall back toward the front room, I heard Grandma's door open upstairs and then the wood floors creaked on the landing.

After turning around in a full circle, I decided to hide in Grandpa's office. I softly closed the door as I heard Grandma coming down the stairs. There was a desk made of burled wood with a small glass lamp on top and a perfect hiding space underneath. I tucked myself in and waited.

A sliver of light came under the door, and I heard water running in the kitchen, the only bulb I didn't unscrew because the chair wasn't high enough to reach the light fixture.

Great. Knowing Grandma, she probably saw the mud and was about to mop for the next six hours. Then I'd be stuck.

Just as I was planning my escape out the window, there was a soft knock on the door.

"Come on out," she said.

Surprised, I uncurled myself from under the desk and stood up, brushing at the snarls in my hair. I opened the door and stood with my hand on my hip and my chin held high like it was perfectly normal to be hiding in Grandpa's office at three o'clock in the morning. "Are you spying on me?"

She looked down at the mud, which led right to the door. "You left a map."

"I forgot to take off my boots."

"It happens. I'll leave the mop and bucket out for you to clean up tomorrow."

Drat.

"Can't sleep?" Grandma said as she walked into the kitchen.

I leaned against the doorway as the teakettle started to wail. She poured the steaming water into a mug. A box of Earl Grey sat beside a plastic bear of honey. She looked comfortable in a fluffy blue robe and plaid flannel pajama bottoms, her long gray-blond hair in a braid.

"Mama drank Earl Grey," I said without meaning to.

Grandma nodded and looked toward the mudroom. My muddy tracks were all over the place. "What were you doing out there?"

"Um. I was missing a sock. I checked in the dryer."

"In the middle of the night?"

"I was bored."

She nodded like that was perfectly understandable. "I've been thinking about the toolbox," Grandma said. "Specifically, the bird you found in there."

I stood up straight, worried. "You can't have it back."

"Of course not. No. I was thinking you could work on it. Finish it for her."

"Are you crazy? It's Mama's."

"I thought we'd both like to have it. Something she made."

"There's no way I could make it look the way she would have. I'd rather keep it the way it is."

There was a long silence as Grandma put the box of tea bags and honey away in the pantry. "Neither one of us was counting on this, Grace. But don't you think we owe it to your mama, to each other, to try?"

"You owe Mama things you can't give me."

"I know I do," she said quietly.

Which took me by surprise.

She leaned against the counter and brought the mug to her lips, blowing at the steam, just the way Mama had. Sometimes, when the light was dim and Grandma turned her head just the right way, I'd get a glimpse of Mama and the sting was something awful.

"Mrs. Greene told me you're a writer," Grandma said. "I'd like to read your work sometime. If it's not too private."

"Well, it is," I said.

"Okay." She looked at me evenly.

I squirmed under her gaze. "I don't understand why you won't let me live with Mrs. Greene. It's not like you want me here."

"If I didn't want you here, you wouldn't be here."

"You're my only next of kin. That's what Mrs. Greene said. So you don't have a choice."

"Everyone has a choice."

I was so mixed up. The person I'd made up Grandma to be, someone hard and cruel, just didn't match this woman who stood across from me. She had summer-blue eyes, like mine and Mama's, and the wrinkles at the outside of those eyes squinched up, like she'd done a lot of laughing in her life. She was graceful in the way she moved between the plants in her yard, caring for each one and giving them what they needed to be healthy and strong. She liked books and I'd seen some of the titles on her shelves: *To Kill a Mockingbird*, *The Secret Life of Bees*, *The Bean Trees*. They didn't look like the kinds of books a mean person might read. I'd even snuck in her room when I'd first gotten here, the only place she kept color, and found a knitted afghan done in purples at the bottom of her bed, a quilt made from floral fabrics, and more books on her nightstand. There was an overstuffed, comfy chair made from bright green fabric, the color of grass, and watercolor paintings on her walls. Trees in winter. An old barn that looked like the one out in the pasture. A golden retriever lying at the base of a chair, a man's boots nearby. I didn't understand why Grandma had to keep the fanciful part of herself, if there really was one, behind a closed door.

"So you're saying you want me here?"

"Of course I do. You're my granddaughter."

But I didn't know how to believe her, how to undo the last twelve years.

Grandma said, "How about you stay in the house tonight. It's almost morning. We can get an early start on pancakes before school."

This wasn't turning out the way it was supposed to. She was supposed to be mad, mad enough to start thinking about sending me back to Mrs. Greene. Instead she was offering to make pancakes. I didn't answer. Instead, I turned around and ran back to the shed.

After school on Thursday, there was a letter from Lacey stuck into the shed door. My first letter! I rushed through my duties in the shed, stoking the fire and checking the rain bucket. Then I wrapped in Mama's quilt on the sofa and tore it open.

82

Dear Grace,

You would not believe what Marsha Trett has done now. She actually asked Denny to the Spring Formal. Can you believe the nerve of her? Was she raised in a barn? Does she not have a decent mother telling her that it's the boy's place to ask the girl to the dance?

I'm sorry to have to tell you that Denny said yes. I thought you should know because I'm never going to talk about him again and now you'll know why. Plus, anyone who would go anywhere with Marsha Trett isn't worth a second thought. Right?

I'm wearing the green sweater you picked out for me. Did I ever tell you that every time I wear it, people tell me it really makes my eyes pop? Then all I can think about are random cartoons where the character's eyes literally pop out of their skulls. So then I giggle. I've always giggled when this happens, but now Marsha has started calling me stuck-up because I can't take a compliment. As if THAT isn't the pot calling the kettle a midget, or whatever that saying is.

I thought of something else for Plan B. I read that if you blow out the pilot light on the water heater (just in case you were wondering why I included a picture of a water heater. It should be in the garage or near the kitchen somewhere) you have to get some special person to come out and turn it on again. Good luck!

*Any idea if your grandma will be getting a computer?
E-mailing would be so much easier and I could totally
write to you fifty times a day! I miss you so much and
can't wait to talk to you. Ten o'clock on Saturday
morning. Not a minute later!!*

Love,

Lacey

I tucked the letter into the Kerr jar next to the Threads
postcard and origami, itching to write things down in my
notebook. I'd learned early that writing worked like that
little hole in the teakettle where steam came pouring out.
I could pour all my steam onto the page, along with my
crazy notions about the world. But every time I looked at
that blank page in my notebook, I just couldn't get myself
to write in the After.

I wrapped tighter into Mama's quilt, looking through
the jar at Lacey's letter, reminding me of everything I'd
lost from Before, and at the Threads postcard that I hoped
might be a way to get me back. Mama was out there somewhere, trying to help, and the possibilities of what might
happen flew around my head, pecking like birds.

I tried reading Frost poems so I could relax. Sometimes I could conjure my father with Mr. Frost's words.
It didn't happen all the time. But once in a great while,
when I wasn't even trying, I could see him there plain as

day, moving around doing some dull task like sweeping the floor or hammering a nail. I tried to conjure him since I didn't know how to do that with Mama yet.

I chose "Reluctance," since that was Daddy's favorite and the poem where Mama found my name.

> Ah, when to the heart of man
>> Was it ever less than a treason
> To go with the drift of things,
>> To yield with a grace to reason,
> And bow and accept the end
>> Of a love or a season?

But no one came.

I refused to give up, though, and eventually, I didn't see Daddy, but I could almost hear Mama's husky voice speaking the words alongside me, making a harmony. If I worked hard enough at following the clues, maybe I could bring all of her back and God would admit a mistake.

As long as I didn't write the After, anything was possible.

10

Worldly Perspective

The reality of these last few weeks, of Mama being gone, down deep in the earth at Fox Hill Cemetery, was still there, but there had to be more than the deep dark earth after you died. Not that I'd given it much thought. Mama and I weren't ones for church, although we had snuck into a few when they'd come across our path. Like when we drove all the way to Tiburon from Turlock on one of our Getaway Days—days where she just had to be somewhere else, so I'd skip school and off we'd go—and found this tiny white-steepled church sitting on a hillside of straw-colored grass. I swore I'd go back and get married in that church one day, and we must have sat there for a good hour, me lying on the pew with my head in Mama's lap, soaking up the stained glass light.

I didn't know how these things worked and it was making me nervous. What if God was looking the other way or something while she sent me signs? Mama was known to be sneaky from time to time, like when she'd crave fresh-baked cookies. If we didn't have the ingredients, or the money for a store run, she'd let herself into whatever diner she worked in, in the wee hours of the night, and bake. Twirling a spatula and listening to the cook's radio turned down low, she'd sing along with the music, humming when she didn't know the words, while I ate chocolate chips and pretended it was our kitchen in a big farmhouse out in the country. With horses.

I hated to think Mama was being sneaky, that if she got caught up there in heaven by the angel police, or whoever was in charge of such things, it might all end. Because it couldn't end. Not until I figured out what she was trying to tell me. I couldn't wait to talk to Lacey tomorrow morning so she could help me sort things out.

On the way to school, Grandma asked me what my favorite subjects were after my first week. She was wearing her gardening uniform again: dirty knee pads and overalls, the same blue bandana holding back her wavy hair.

"I guess they would be art and English."

"Art was one of your mama's favorite subjects," Grandma said, and I wondered if she'd ever stop telling me things as though I didn't know my own mama.

"You should do the laundry today. Looks like you've

been wearing the same clothes all week," I said, thinking about the soap-bubble mess that was waiting for her and trying not to crack up.

"I already did the laundry."

"You did?" I said, confused, since I'd switched the soaps two days ago.

"I did."

I couldn't read Grandma's face. Was she trying not to laugh?

"Well," I said. "How did it go?"

"It went the way laundry always goes. Everything got clean."

I didn't know what to make of that as I got out of the truck and ran up the front sidewalk to school, my back-pack bumping against my side.

I'd managed to keep my distance from Jo and the other girls for most of this first week, although I saw them huddle from time to time and look in my direction, like they might be hatching a plan. My plan, however, was to walk wide circles around everyone like they had something catching, chicken pox, maybe, or a really bad case of bedbugs. This way I could stay focused on Mama's treasure-hunt clues.

Mrs. Snickels wanted our self-portrait sketches fin-ished, so when I got into third period a little early, I took out my portrait right away and went to work. I was coming to love art, as much as I could love anything anymore. The smell of paint and the mess of Mrs. Snickels's desk were comforting, and I could feel Mama in the quiet way everyone worked. It was almost like being with her. Almost.

Just as the final bell rang, Jo slammed into the room, blowing away my peaceful thoughts, with Beth and Ginger following close behind. Ginger was all in black today, making me think even more about mimes. Jo dropped her backpack on the floor beside her stool, and Beth and Ginger sat at their own table, murmuring to each other. Beth's T-shirt read, A TIDY ROOM IS A HAPPY ROOM.

After much whispering, Beth came over and put a pink-fingernailed hand on Jo's shoulder. Beth's hair was neatly French braided, and I wondered if her mother had done it for her. "Listen, Jo, things will definitely be okay in the end, and if it isn't okay, it isn't the end."

"Whatever, Beth."

"Don't 'whatever' me. I'm just trying to be helpful."

"Don't you ever think that maybe I don't want your help? Maybe I just want to, I don't know, figure it out myself. In fact, why don't you make me a label that says LEAVE ME ALONE and I'll stick it to my forehead."

Beth's perfectly glossed lips formed a tiny round O, like the idea of being alone had never occurred to her in the entirety of her life. "You don't mean that."

Jo looked straight at her and said in a low, serious voice, "You guys have no idea what this has been like."

"This isn't just happening to you, Jo. Did you ever think of that?"

Beth stormed away, her long, billowy scarf trailing behind her.

"At least I'm not a walking self-help poster," Jo said.

Beth and Ginger went back to whispering until Mrs. Snickels came and stood over their shoulders. Eventually, they quieted down and took out their work.

I figured it was none of my business, so I kept drawing.

Jo sniffed. "In case you were wondering what all the drama is about, Max just threw a fit because he couldn't find his red suitcase. He accused his best friend of hiding it and they got in a huge fight. He was inconsolable and Mom had to come pick him up. Then they found the suitcase in the stupid coat closet, but she took him home anyway."

I wasn't sure if she wanted me to say anything. But after her third dramatic sigh, I gave up on my sketch for the time being. "He must have had a good reason. People don't usually blame their best friends for stuff unless there's a reason for it."

"I guess you're going to find out how weird we are sooner or later." Jo put her head in her hands and talked down at the table. "Max wraps himself in bandages, like a mummy. He insists he isn't going to stop until we give him an entombment party, and his friends are teasing him. There, I said it."

I remembered his bandaged hands on the first day of school and seeing him and Jo talking to Grandma at the pasture fence before that. Talk about commitment.

"That's pretty brave," I said.

"Hmph."

Mama had always told me it was a good deed to help when I could, to share my worldly perspective, having met so many people along the way. "Don't let any part of yourself go to waste, Gracie May," she'd say. I supposed it wouldn't hurt.

"I've seen boys do weirder things," I offered.

"You could not possibly have seen anything weirder than an eight-year-old boy who wraps himself in gauze bandages—which he pays for out of his own allowance, I should add—and insists he will keep doing it until we throw him a death party."

"I knew this kid named Timmy Parker who swore his mother killed his friend Wrinkle by dropping a bag of groceries on his head."

Jo looked up from the table. "You are making that up."

I shook my head. "Nope. Wrinkle was his imaginary friend, but Timmy wouldn't admit it. His mother didn't even know what she'd done. She was just setting a bag of groceries on the backseat of the car. Timmy carried on and on about how no one would bury Wrinkle. Told everyone the rotting corpse was giving him nightmares. Spent half the time in the nurse's office claiming he had post-traumatic stress disorder. His father was a psychiatrist."

Jo had one elbow propped, her chin resting in her hand. She didn't look quite so down, like a balloon half-filled.

"So our teacher, Mrs. Lemon, went ahead and gave Wrinkle a proper burial with a eulogy and everything. We dug a hole in the second-grade vegetable garden and laid Wrinkle to rest between the tomatoes and the lettuce. Timmy turned into a regular kid after that."

Jo pulled her portrait out of the storage tube. "Max will never be a regular kid."

"Sometimes people have to do weird things before they're regular," I said.

"How much weird do we have to put up with?"

"I suppose it's different for everyone."

She thought for a minute. "That was a good story."

Figuring my good deed was done, I went back to sketching just as Stubbie came rushing toward me with a piece of drawing paper in his hand, Archer chasing after. Stubbie threw the paper down in front of me, and I saw a sketch of myself looking out a big window, one hand up to the glass, and smiling at something on the other side. It was as though Archer had drawn me into one of Mr. Frost's poems. It made me want to climb inside so I might feel what she was feeling.

"It's not you," Archer said. "It's my cousin Wanda."

"You don't have a cousin Wanda," Stubbie said.

Everyone in the class sat there, quiet, giving a moment of silence to the death of Archer's dignity, but all I wanted to do was ask him if he'd actually seen that girl—had I even smiled in the last five days?—or dreamed her up. I felt a flush come up my cheeks as I noticed Archer's eyes and how unusual they were, almond shaped and a light grayish green.

After the moment passed, Jo got busy ignoring us, and Stubbie went back to their table, snickering. Archer was suddenly composed, like he might launch into his own Shakespearean monologue instead of Ginger. Which, if he did, would be the most spectacular form of diversion I'd ever seen.

"May I please have my sketch back?" he asked instead.

I handed it to him, sad to see it go, and he went to his desk, where he punched Stubbie in the arm. Stubbie grabbed his arm and pretended to be seriously injured, making faces, sticking out his tongue, being a general spectacle.

Ginger declared, "The measure of a man is made in moments of discomfort and uncertainty."

Beth nodded and typed something up on her label maker.

"Good heavens, we haven't had this much chaos around here since Mr. Flinch lost Henry VIII and we found the poor little guy in the supply closet," Mrs. Snickels said.

"Henry VIII?" I said to Jo.

"A rat. Mr. Flinch feels that we should always name our class pets after 'rapscallions and historical tyrants.'"

"Someone ought to name a rat after Stubbie Wilkins," I said. Jo looked over at him and he raised his bushy red eyebrows, up and down, up and down.

"He'd probably take it as a compliment," she said.

We shared a smile, and for one slippery moment, I felt like my Before self.

My prowling around at night and general sleeplessness finally must have caught up with me, because I fell asleep in Mr. Flinch's class. I woke up with the rest of the seats empty. Talk about an *Alice in Wonderland* moment.

The first thing I saw was an origami crane made from newspaper on the bookshelf beside me, which then made me feel even more disoriented. Like I'd dreamed a bird into being. It sat on a stack of newspapers, blending in.

I wiped the drool from my cheek, mortified, and looked up to see Mr. Flinch grading papers. The banana clock over his head read twelve thirty-five. I'd slept through his fourth-period social studies class, and into lunch.

"Has this always been here?" I said, pointing to the crane.

"Ah! Another country heard from! Did you sleep well?"

"Why didn't you wake me up?"

"We didn't have the heart. Stubbie Wilkins suggested we get out the indelible markers, but he is a heathen."

Great. Every single seventh-grader saw me drooling all over my desk. "Did I snore?"

"Ha! No. You are a very quiet sleeper."

He was tall and thin, his legs stilt-like as he crossed the room toward me. He wore sweaters with elbow patches, but in unexpected colors, like sage or plum. Jo had told me he'd taught Shakespeare at a really big college on the East Coast, but he gave it up because he "preferred shaping the clay of young minds" and "left his heart in Auburn Valley," as he'd grown up here himself. He and Ginger sometimes launched into dueling Shakespearean monologues. His were probably real. But if I was being fair, Ginger had something going for her in that way good actresses did. There was something about her that made you pay attention. Plus she was goofy.

I picked up the crane and looked it over. It was smaller than the one from the bushes.

"It's probably an extra," Mr. Flinch said, nodding toward the little bird.

"An extra?"

"May I?" he said.

I handed him the crane.

"Do you know anything about origami?"

I shook my head and used my sweatshirt to wipe the

little puddle of drool I'd gotten on the desk. He handed me his handkerchief in a well-folded square and pointed to my chin, where I'd missed a spot.

He went back to his desk, where he took out a piece of canary-yellow paper. Then he sat down next to me and began to fold.

"Each year, we talk about Sadako and her thousand paper cranes. Sadako was a girl who lived in Japan during World War II. She was two when the atom bomb dropped on Hiroshima, leveling everything. She lived for ten years before getting sick with radiation poisoning."

"Did she die?"

He nodded, still folding. "There's a Japanese legend that says if you fold one thousand paper cranes, you get a wish. Sadako started folding and got to six hundred and forty-four, but didn't finish, and so the children she went to school with finished for her."

"That's really sad."

"Today, from all around the world, people send batches of one thousand paper cranes to Japan as a gesture of peace."

Mr. Flinch folded and folded and eventually an origami crane sat perched in his hand. Like magic. "There are some who say this town was founded on the luck of a crane."

"I thought people came here for the gold."

"They did. But it's said that a man—a lone miner who had traveled the world in search of his fortune and, while doing so, lost his one and only love—came to California during the gold rush. He strayed away from others who were working farther down the hill, and when he came upon a crane at Wolf Creek, he stopped, taking it for a sign of luck. He discovered what ended up being the richest mine in California, married again, and had ten daughters. You won't find that in the history books, but the story has come down over generations. If you look, you can find cranes in odd places."

He set the bird down on the desk in front of me.

"My mama believed that birds were a signpost, and if you needed it, they might just point the way."

"Your mother was in good company with her beliefs. The crane is a mystical bird. Some think it carries souls up to heaven on its outstretched wings. Some believe it signifies healing and hope." He tapped its wing. "That's a lot of responsibility for a little bird, wouldn't you say?"

I nodded.

"Feel free to take them both. I'm sorry you missed the lesson. It is always quite inspirational."

I tried to hand him his handkerchief.

"Keep that too. One never knows when one might need a handkerchief for dramatic flair."

11

Three
Small Bites

After I started writing in my notebooks, I realized the poems Mama had been reading to me out of *A Boy's Will* weren't just pretty words, but they actually made some kind of sense. When I asked her to help me piece them together, she put a finger to my forehead and told me that some people had to learn to think and other people had to learn to un-think, and I was one of the last kind. *Thinking can steal the magic right out of a thing. The trick is finding a good balance.* She went on to tell me that those poems were like colorful bits of laundry all pinned to a line and blowing in the breeze. *Let the pictures come from the words, Grace. It's the seeing that stays with you. You might see something different on a different day.*

Later I'd told her that was why we made a good team. She believed in magic, and I liked to think, so between the two of us, we had it covered. She'd laughed and told me she'd find a way, someday, to make me see the magic of a thing. Now, I figured, she was having her way.

Before crawling into my sleeping bag, I put the two new origami cranes—the one made out of newspaper, and the yellow one Mr. Flinch had made—into the Kerr jar. Then I took out the unfinished crane from Mama's toolbox, pressing my finger into one of the sharp corners until there was a dent in the pad of my finger. I thought about Grandma wanting me to finish it, but I didn't know if I could find the heart for it. I didn't know how to choose the pieces. Plus I couldn't decide which would be better— leaving it as is or finishing it in the likeness of the others Mama had made, as a tribute to her.

I tucked the bird under my pillow, hoping the answer might come in my dreams. If I might have some good ones for a change.

As I went running out the shed door in the morning, excited for my Lacey call, I noticed the Brannigans' stormy-sky horse stood at the fence across the pasture as she did most mornings. She neighed and shook her head from side to side. Because I was feeling generous after my recent discoveries, I went back and grabbed an uneaten apple out of my backpack and trudged across the high weeds of the pasture, getting my jeans wet with dew.

Mrs. Brannigan drove their white truck down the driveway on the far side of their pasture, Max and Jo beside her. She stopped and the window rolled down. "We're headed to Spoons; do you want to come?"

Jo wore a black beret and small round sunglasses. She leaned over her brother and yelled, "I'm doing an interview for the documentary. Beth flaked and I could use some help!"

"I've got stuff to do," I called, hiding the apple behind my back. "Sorry."

With a wave from all three, Mrs. Brannigan rolled the window up and turned right onto Ridge Road. I watched them disappear from view before heading the rest of the way to the fence.

I'd never fed a horse before and realized with a shudder that my whole arm could fit in her mouth. But I was committed, so I figured I'd just do it the way I'd seen it done on some animal show on TV. I put out my hand, flat, and she brought her muzzle down, her lips like velvet across my skin as they gathered up the apple. She had big teeth.

After she finished, she nudged my hand for more. "Sorry, girl. Besides, it looks like you've been eating plenty."

I patted her round belly through the wire fence, and then her belly kicked my hand. I pulled back, startled. Once I realized what I'd felt, I pressed both hands against her belly, where I felt more movement. A baby.

I stood there and stroked her nose until her eyes were

droopy, imagining being connected to Mama that way. There was a sudden rush of sadness that got so big, I was sure it would munch me up in three small bites.

Tiny drops of fine mist covered Grandma's bun-tight head, caught there the way mist will catch in a spider's web. She had just come in from the garden, of course. The table was set with plain white dishes and jelly jars for juice glasses. There were white cloth napkins, small bowls of brown sugar and raisins, and the bear-shaped bottle of honey. The newspaper sat next to Grandma's plate, and beside the newspaper was a family-sized box of latex gloves.

"Morning," Grandma said. She took a pot off the stove and set it on an orange knitted hot pad, eyeglasses swinging on a chain around her neck. "I understand you have a phone call this morning."

"In fifteen minutes," I said.

"Later this afternoon, I've got a delivery of manure coming, and I could use some help with it," Grandma said.

"Manure? Really?"

"Really."

"What time?"

"Around one. Why? Do you have plans?"

I couldn't tell if she sounded hopeful or if it was just

a pesky question. Either way, one o'clock didn't give me much time to get to town, investigate Threads and Margery, and get back.

"I've got homework."

"Well, you can get to that after the manure. Maybe you can bring it back here to the kitchen. Your mama used to do her homework right there where you're sitting."

I laid my hands on the hard wood of the chair while Grandma served us each a heaping bowl of oatmeal. Then she sat down and snapped on the little rubber gloves. I'd seen enough television to know that criminals wore those little gloves when they didn't want to leave fingerprints behind. For a second, I thought I might be a goner, that maybe she'd figured out about Plan B.

She caught me looking at her all goggle-eyed but didn't say a word. Instead, she popped open her newspaper as though all the world wore rubber gloves to the breakfast table.

"Something interesting happened a couple of days ago," Grandma said.

"My laundry detergent was replaced with dish soap. Good thing I caught it, or we would have had an explosion of bubbles."

"Good thing," I said, studying a crack in the wood table.

"And all my lightbulbs were unscrewed."

"Really?" I said.

"Are you really going to pretend you don't know what I'm talking about?"

I looked up, suddenly furious. "Why would you think I did it?"

Grandma gestured out the bay window. "Although they have been known to get into mischief, the raccoons around here probably aren't taking my laundry detergent or unscrewing lightbulbs."

I crossed my arms and huffed. "How do you know? I've read about cats taking people's shoes. That's weirder."

This was not going the way it was supposed to. She was supposed to be spitting mad, not half-amused. Because once she was good and mad, I could own up to it so she would know I was a nuisance. Then I was supposed to keep being a nuisance until she gave up on me and sent me back to Mrs. Greene's. But her blaming me, just assuming that I could be a nuisance without any proof, made *me* spitting mad. After all, I wasn't the type of kid who usually did pokey, bothersome things. It was her fault I'd stooped so low.

"Well, I can only hope the raccoons don't organize a coup," she said.

I could tell she was looking at me, but I wouldn't raise

my eyes from the oatmeal. After a while she went back to reading the current events. "The horse's name is Beauty," she said.

That got my eyes up. "You are spying on me!"

"Nonsense. I was in the side garden this morning and saw you two in the front pasture."

I had decided not to talk to her for the rest of breakfast. But then I couldn't help myself. "Is she going to have a baby?"

"Soon, I believe."

I picked at my oatmeal.

"You're still not eating."

"I'm not hungry. Plus I don't like oatmeal. Did you ever have horses?"

Grandma's newspaper crinkled. "We never did. Dogs, but no horses. Why didn't you tell me before about the oatmeal?" She got up and popped a piece of bread in the toaster, fussing with crumbs on the counter.

"Did you have a golden retriever?"

She stopped fussing and looked at me. "You've been in my room."

Double drat. I had to think more before I talked. "No. I just saw the painting through the open door."

Grandma sat down. "The door is never open. You like toast, I presume."

"Fine. I snooped in your room. Did you really think I wouldn't?"

She smiled and I could see Mama. "I suppose not. All kids are snoops. Me too. I've been out in your grandfather's woodshop."

I was immediately furious again and then realized how silly that was. Of course she snooped.

"So then why did you ask to read my writing when you obviously have already?"

"I didn't read your notebooks. Some things are private."

Mama had always said that people give clues about themselves in everything they do and say and that it was a good idea to keep track so you knew if someone's feet went in the same direction as their flapping lips, which was a fancy way of saying their actions matched their words. So far, Grandma hadn't said all that many words, but most of her actions were kind. Like respecting the privacy of my notebooks and buying me new clothes. If I didn't know she'd sent Mama on a bus to Texas, I would have figured her for a nice person.

"The golden retriever from the painting? His name was Willie Mays," Grandma said.

"You named your dog Willie Mays?" I got up and buttered my own toast. She sat back down.

"Yes, we named our dog Willie Mays. Your grandpa

was a San Francisco Giants fan. Willie would moon for hours whenever your mama and grandpa went birding." She gestured down the hall toward the front windows. "He used to sit there and wait for them to come home."

A stillness came over her then, as though she might have said too much. I recognized it from my own efforts to stay clammed up.

"What are you going to do after you talk to Lacey?" Grandma said, changing the subject.

"Just my homework. It's, um, a seriously time-consuming project. It's going to take me a very long time. So long, in fact, I might just miss the whole manure extravaganza."

Grandma looked over the tops of her half-glasses. "What subject?"

Flailing around for the first project to cross my mind, I said, "Art. Um . . . I'm helping Jo with her documentary."

"Jo from next door?" She smiled as though that made her happy.

The idea blossomed in fabulous colors. "Yes! I'm supposed to meet her at Spoons to help!"

"Well, for heaven's sake, why didn't you say so before?"

"I . . . forgot."

The grandfather clock in the front room clanged the hour. It was ten o'clock. Time for my call to Lacey.

"Go ahead," Grandma said.

I ran into Grandpa's office, shutting the door carefully, thinking how Grandma and I had an entire conversation and it didn't actually kill me. I sat down and pulled the old green phone toward me. Then I dialed Lacey and Mrs. Greene, bouncy in Grandpa's big leather chair.

After four rings, I got their answering machine. After five more tries, I realized they weren't home. After another half hour of calling every few minutes, I realized they must have forgotten about me already.

I was on my own.

12

The Great
Beyond

After I pulled myself together, I came out of the office and walked down the hall.

"Everything okay?" Grandma called.

"They weren't home," I said. "I left a message."

Grandma got up to stand in the kitchen doorway. "Does Mrs. Greene have a cell phone you could try?"

"I did."

"Oh. I'm sure they must have a good reason."

I reached the front door.

"I'll give you a ride into town."

"I'd rather ride my bike."

"Can I at least pick you up? It's looking like it might rain."

"I've got a coat."

"Are you sure?"

"Yes! Just leave me alone!" I slammed out the door.

Walking back to the shed, I worried there'd been an accident. I pictured Mrs. Greene and Lacey lying beneath matching flowered sheets, the same kind of sheet I'd taken off the bed to cover Mama after I'd found her. I shook my head and cleared those thoughts away.

It took me ten minutes to get down the trail on my bike. Main Street consisted of two blocks of buildings, some painted in pastels, others weathered redbrick with white block lettering, everything faded, like the whole town had been washed and dried too many times. An old two-story hotel sat on the corner opposite the Spoons Souperie, built during the gold rush, or so the plaque claimed. The hotel was all that was left of fancier times. Everything else was more practical. Lafollette's Market. Cakery Bakery. Threads.

I stopped outside Margery's storefront, where there was a display of four mannequins, two wearing sheer nighties alongside two in flannel nightgowns—all four in hideous wigs. A spring scene with stuffed bunnies, Easter basket grass, and the kind of colored plastic eggs that snap open so they can be filled with sugary candies lay at their slippered feet. I leaned my bike against the brick wall and looked past the window display into the store beyond.

Margery was behind the counter. The dim light from the overcast day barely reached where she sat with her nose buried in paperwork. She wore a muumuu with a mix of frantic colors that would give anyone a headache if they stared too long, and the same straw cowboy hat she'd worn at Mama's funeral. Even from this distance, I could see her silver-and-turquoise rings, one on each finger.

Hanging on the high brick wall behind her was a sign made from found objects. The *T* in *Threads* was an extra-large gardening trowel and a rough piece of reclaimed wood. It looked like something Mama would have made.

Margery noticed me gawking and waved for me to come inside.

The cold came inside with me and then died at my feet. There was a wood stove going in the corner. Where I expected lavender, or some other panty-drawer kind of scent, it smelled like the freshly ground coffee beans and baked goods from the bakery next door. My stomach rumbled, the first time I'd noticed I had a stomach in forever.

"About time you got your skinny butt in here," Margery said.

I nodded toward the sign behind her. "Did Mama make that?"

"Well, hello to you too," Margery said. She swiveled toward the wall and looked up. "Nope. Your father did."

"My . . . father?"

She motioned to a large antique bureau, drawers part-way open, with bras and panties stacked neatly on display. On top were silver framed photos. At least twenty. I picked up one of the heavy frames. Mama and Daddy in the daisy meadow. I couldn't believe it. It was exactly the same as mine. I wanted to ask about a million questions but I had no idea where to start.

"Good heavens. Do your underthings look as horrid as your outer things?"

As I looked down at my sweatshirt and jeans under the open peacoat, I considered feeling insulted, but she was right. It had been a while since I'd had new clothes.

Margery scurried about the rows of bras and picked three. They were delicate, with a bit of lace edging at the bottom. Nothing you'd ever find at the dollar store.

"Try these," she commanded.

I stood there holding the bras in one hand, the picture in the other, not sure what to do first: ask questions or try on the bras. Finally, I figured I could do both so I hurried behind a red velvet curtain that closed off a changing area and choked something out. "How did you know him . . . my father?"

"He lived in the little guesthouse out back of my property."

I took off Mama's peacoat and laid it on an overstuffed leopard-print chair, setting the picture carefully on top. Turning my back to the mirror, I lifted my sweatshirt over my head. I hooked the bra as quickly as I could, feeling self-conscious under the soft yellow light. I turned around.

Instead of seeing the bra, I saw bags under my eyes, the

points of both hip bones above my jeans, and every single rib. I looked like the zombie I'd tried to be for Mrs. Greene and didn't recognize myself.

Mama and Daddy peered up at me from the frame. They probably didn't recognize me either.

"Fit?" Margery asked. "What am I saying? Of course it does. I'm never wrong about the fit. Hand me the other two."

I looked at the price tags. Thirty dollars each!

"Um . . . I don't have any money . . ."

"Of course you don't," Margery said. "Consider them a very late baby gift."

I dressed quickly and came out, holding the picture tight to my chest. "Are you sure? Because I could work them off." Mama didn't like taking charity.

"You come in here and talk to me. That will be payment enough."

I surprised myself by smiling, then laid the picture on the counter as I sat on a nearby stool. "What was he like?" I said.

"Didn't your mama tell you about him?"

I shook my head. "She didn't like to talk about things that made her sad."

"Of course she didn't. But a girl has a right to know her daddy." Margery gestured toward the bureau. "Second drawer from the left."

I went where she pointed and pulled out a stack of multicolored flyers—blue, green, yellow—wrinkled, dog-eared, and smudged with dirt. They advertised the grand opening of the Bear River Park.

"Your dad helped me here," Margery said.

"Here?"

"Well, he didn't fold bras if that's what you're thinking. He oiled the hinges on the door, built shelves. He put up the baseboards and painted for me. That sort of thing. If you explained what you wanted, he could draw you a picture and then build it."

"How long did he live on your property?"

"Two years. He came to town when he was sixteen after his parents died in a house fire. I was a family friend."

There were times I'd looked at the picture of Daddy and Mama and think about what he might have been like. He had a soothing voice and a big vocabulary, and even though he was quite a chef and could make anything with a French name, he liked hamburgers and onion rings most of all. He would wear denim work shirts and carry a paintbrush in his back pocket. He would have a silly nickname for me like Snub or Shorty. I'd made him up from top to bottom and it was weird to hear Margery explain this entirely different person. A stranger.

She went on to tell me that he and Mama had run smack into each other right in front of the shop his second day in town, knocking themselves into a heap. Mama had been carrying the load of Bear River Park flyers, which took off for the heavens on what had been a blustery day. Margery said those flyers floated about town for weeks, and each time Scott found one, he stuffed it in the drawer, falling more and more in love with her each time. Margery never had the heart to toss them out.

"That was the kind of kid he was. Saving every scrap of paper. Every little bit of nothing. That's what losing everything can do if you let it." Margery took off one cowboy boot and then the other, rubbing her toes through purple socks. I rested my elbows on the counter. "Your mother was just what he needed. Swimming in the river with snow on the ground. Climbing trees because the view was better. Raging at the sky when a deer got himself hit out on Ridge Road. She was one big beating heart, that girl, and it helped him open up again."

One big beating heart. That was Mama.

"Was he strong?" I said. I'd always imagined a daddy who could lift me onto his shoulders.

"He was wiry strong, not beefy strong."

"Did he like to give hugs?"

"I don't think he let go of your mom from the minute he met her."

"How did you know his family?"

"Before I came up here and opened my shop, I lived

in San Diego. I owned a little store on the water, sort of like this one, and your daddy's parents owned the one next door. Rare and used books. Your daddy was a surfer and a bookworm all the days of his life. His favorite candies were these little butterscotches from a store on the same boardwalk, so I'd keep a bowl of them behind the counter just for him. When he was small, he'd zoom in, all bare feet and sunburned nose, covered in sand, and sneak behind my counter for the candy, embarrassed about the bras and underwear. When he got older, though, he'd walk in all cool and collected, sometimes putting on one of my frill-iest bras over his own shirt and posing in the mirror. He was quite a character."

"I was born in San Diego," I said. "Was my dad born there too?"

"He was."

I let the heart of him sink in while at the same time try-ing not to be mad at Margery. She knew everything about him and I could only know things she saw fit to tell me. I wished I could zoom around her brain and pick up the knickknacks of his life, one at a time.

But I supposed it wasn't her fault. Besides, it was more than Mama had ever said. She didn't even tell me she'd picked San Diego to have me because that was where my father had been born, if that was even the reason.

As more questions flooded my mind, the front door

opened and closed, ruffling the yellow feather boa hanging behind Margery.

"Is she here?" Grandma's voice. "I saw the bike . . ."

"Miranda! It's good to see you."

I turned around.

Grandma's face was gray as the sky outside. She reached for the arm of a zebra-print chair and sat down, out of breath, putting a hand to her silver cross. What in the world was she doing here?

Margery looked from Grandma to me and back to Grandma again. She put her hands on her good-sized hips. "Good Lord, did you take off without telling your grandma where you were going?"

"I ran into Mrs. Brannigan in the driveway," Grandma said to me. "When I asked her how things were going with you and Jo at Spoons, she didn't know what I was talking about."

Margery swept by and grabbed a crystal pitcher off the bureau, tsking at me, and poured Grandma a glass of water. "Of all the things you could have done."

Grandma took the water, and I felt bad for making her worry. She seemed so fragile sitting there, all pale and worked up. She was a person with feelings, I supposed. I studied my worn sneakers, the dirty and frayed shoelaces.

"I got . . . sidetracked," I said.

Grandma stood up, brushing at a smudge of dirt on her pants. "I'll wait outside."

There, she took my bike from where it was leaning against the wall and loaded it into the back of Granny Smith.

"Your grandma might look like she's made of wood, but she's not." Margery put my bras in a white bag covered in red kisses. "Try and keep that in mind the next time you think about going somewhere without telling her."

Margery had turned stiff, and I had to make it up to her. She was my only connection to Daddy, plus I had come for an important reason. I reached in my pocket and took out the postcard. "I found this in Mama's things. Do you know what it might mean?"

She looked it over and then read the back. "*A Secret Meadow.* Hmmmm. Could mean this place." She pointed to the daisies in the picture of Mama and Daddy on the counter. "I don't know where it is, though, sugar. The one with the answers is probably that lady standing right outside. You might want to start with her."

The picture of Mama and Daddy in the meadow. That was why it had seemed so familiar.

Grandma knocked on the window and pointed to her watch. The thought of her beloved manure probably helped her get back some composure.

"Are you and Grandma friends?"

"For my part." Margery seemed to soften again. "Listen, you come back and visit me. I'd like to know what you've been up to for the last twelve years. I've missed your mama." She slipped the flyers Daddy had collected all those years ago into the bag. "There's something to remember your daddy by. I'll dig around and see what else I can find."

I thanked her and agreed to come back as soon as I could, then went outside and stood next to Grandma. We watched the sleet come down.

"Spring in the foothills is always unpredictable this time of year," Grandma said.

"I'm hungry."

She looked at me like I'd figured something out. Brain surgery, maybe. Then she reached into her purse, pulled out an umbrella, and handed it to me. "Come on, then."

"What about your manure?"

"There'll be other days for manure."

I turned around and looked over my shoulder. Margery waved and then blew a kiss. I raised my hand in return, wanting to know so much more. I couldn't wait to get back.

Grandma hurried through the sleet and I caught up, holding the umbrella over us both, feeling the new bra under my sweatshirt like a secret.

13

Soup and Mummies

The big spoon hanging overhead made me think of Mama's birds again. She was always taking spoons from the diners she worked in or from flea markets and yard sales to use in her birds.

The front door opened and we were welcomed into the Spoons Souperie by a mummy. A small one. It stood there against the door, tufts of brown hair popping out between its bandages, wearing glasses and holding a giant book.

"It's me, Max," the mummy said, struggling with a large book called *The Egyptian Way of Death*.

Grandma nudged me toward Max and then took a seat at the Formica counter on a red vinyl stool. Her purse sat beside her.

Jo sat in a booth, eating a bowl of soup, her bag of camera equipment on the floor beside her. She waved me over, looking just as glum as she had in art class.

There were two sides to the diner separated by a wide brick-arched opening. Both sides had high ceilings with huge wooden beams stretching from one side to the other and held evidence of the mill it was once upon a time. Rusted saw blades hung on the faded brick walls, and old photographs of serious-looking men standing on logs as thick as the men were tall, their large mustaches hiding sly smiles maybe, as though they knew something I didn't. It reminded me of the diners Mama had worked in. There'd been Cole's Joint, where you ordered your burger by pointing to the buffalo, ostrich, or deer head festooning the wall. Mulligan's, where Mulligan himself played bass on Friday nights. Jeremy's, which served the hottest chili in the state of California and had the pictures of people's whacked-out faces to prove it.

In the other room were lots of tables and comfy-looking mismatched chairs, where a few people sat working at their laptops or reading by the wood stove. The Souperie was busy on this cold day, with a handful of waitresses. One was elderly, small but sturdy, with hair swept back in a poufy white bun. She bustled from here to there, humming. Her name tag said LOU.

Archer Lee Hamilton cleared dishes from one of the booths into a big plastic tub, and when he caught sight of me, he smiled a shy smile, then went back to work. Seeing him there flustered me, which I wouldn't have expected.

"The corn chowder is the best," Max said as I sat across from Jo. He scooted in next to me. A bunch of books were piled on one end of the table, books about hieroglyphics and pharaohs and Egyptian tombs. His red suitcase was propped next to Jo's equipment.

Jo smiled, pulling at the edge of her beret. "He's only eating yellow things at the moment—that's why he's telling you to eat the corn chowder. All the soups are good."

I picked up a menu, spying on Archer as he hurried from one table to the next. There were seven kinds of soup, and fresh-baked bread. That was it. Max and Jo both had mostly empty bowls in front of them, bread plates piled with crusts.

"I like your hat," I said.

"Thanks. My uncle brought it back from France. He said every good director needs to wear a beret."

"Did you find someone to help with the interview?" I said.

"Sure. Archer helped. I just needed to make sure the lighting was set up the right way and that someone watched over the camera while I talked with Lou and Mel. Mel is the cook and Lou is the waitress. They've been married for forty-five years."

"I told you I could have helped," Max grumped.

"You knock things over."

Lou swept by the table to take my order. She had little spindly legs and wore those white rubber-soled shoes you usually saw on a nurse. She had kind eyes and a slight tremor in her writing hand. I ordered matzo ball soup, one of my favorite comfort foods.

"I was sorry to hear about your mama," she said.

Face by face, I was starting to recognize the people from Mama's funeral. I nodded in thanks.

"Did you know she used to steal my spoons for her art?" She said, proud. I shook my head. "I used to order extra for her. Took me a while to get out of the habit."

Lou snatched a lacy kerchief out of her apron pocket and dabbed at her eyes before shouting, "Matzo on one!" and hurrying away.

"Thanks, Lou," Jo called after her. "She's an emotional person. Especially after her and Mel's interview."

"You interviewed them about the park?" I said.

She nodded. "Your grandma designed the pathways and what kinds of plants would go into the park. How big it would be, that sort of thing. But the town council let anyone sponsor a space and submit design plans if they wanted. Lou and Mel built a tree house for their son, Billy. He was killed in the First Gulf War."

I found Lou setting a bowl of steaming soup down on a table across the restaurant. She buzzed back to the kitchen. Then my gaze drifted over to Grandma, who had lost her child too. Now they had that awful thing in common.

"When they found out Billy had died, Mel got to making soup every day as a way of coping. They had soup in the freezer and soup in the fridge. They'd take soup to the neighbors, and finally, Lou decided enough was enough and they bought this place."

Mel poured his sorrow into the soup the way Mama had poured hers into her birds. I held the spoon tight in my hand, wishing I could picture Mama in this place, eating soup in one of the booths and slipping spoons into her bag. Being a regular part of everyone's lives, like the hair on their heads or the smiles on their faces.

"Anyway!" Jo said. "What do you think Mrs. Snickels will have us do on the other half of the self-portrait?"

I shrugged. "Hopefully it won't involve a gong."

She and Max laughed. I smiled. For a brief moment, all the swirling sorrows flew out of reach.

Archer came to the table to drop off my soup, and we had a moment where I felt sure the soup would end up in my lap. Somehow, he managed to right himself, though, and land it on the table with only one small drop leaping out.

"That was a magnificent save," Jo said.

Archer took a deep bow. "And now for my bread performance."

He went into the kitchen and came back with a basket of bread, holding it above his head on one hand. He did a clumsy pirouette just before placing it on the table next to my bowl and perfectly covering the small drop of soup that had escaped. He smoothed his bangs off his forehead and we all clapped.

"How many times have I told you, Archer? No ballet in the restaurant!" Lou called from behind the counter. Then she hooted.

"It wasn't ballet," he called back. "I was square dancing!"

"Well, in that case."

"You are such a goober," Jo said.

"Only when I'm nervous." Archer smiled at me. Before I could say anything back, he scooted away.

I felt the familiar curve of friendship trying to pull me in. It was hard to fight those natural feelings of wanting to settle in, so I let myself rest for a bit. Maybe it was the girlish bra, making me soft.

"What's with the bandages?" I said to Max, poking the bendy straw into my ice water. "Jo says you want to have some kind of entombment party."

"Class project." He slid his eyes toward Jo. "Everyone else is doing a mission. But Ms. White said I could build a pyramid."

"Really?" I said. "And you need to build it in full mummy gear?"

Jo rolled her eyes. "A few weeks ago, we opened this five-year-old jar of apple butter, but it tasted fresh-picked. Tut here figured if he could seal himself up like the apple butter, he'd be preserved in the afterlife."

"That's what the Egyptians did!" Max exclaimed. "But I need an entombment party with all the fixin's so I can live forever in the afterlife too."

Max's book, *The Egyptian Way of Death*, was turned to a particularly interesting page that had to do with brain extraction.

"Can I be the one to slurp your brains out your nose and collect your innards in a pot?" Jo said.

Max spooned up a gelatinous potato from his bowl and thwacked it toward Jo's head. She leaned to the left, and Lou caught it midflight.

"Don't you start a food fight in my restaurant, Max Brannigan," Lou said.

"I won't!" Max said.

Jo looked murderous. She sat up tall. "You are eight years old. I am twelve. I will not be brought down to your level over a chunk of potato."

Max calmly foisted another potato at her, and this one landed, *splat,* under her left eye, leaving a snail trail as it slid down her face.

"You are an imbecile."

"Don't you mean *invalid?*"

Jo wiped at her cheek with a paper napkin. "No, imbecile. I'll be right back, Grace."

I dug in to my soup. It was the best I'd ever had, spiced with sorrow or not, and I ate like the starving person I was.

Max watched me, and after a while he said, "Egyptians were buried with their wordly possessions so they could take them into the afterlife." He reached down and pulled his suitcase into the booth. "I don't want to be alone without my stuff."

"You aren't going to the afterlife anytime soon," I said.

"No one knows when they're going. I could step off the curb and get hit by a bus or fall out of a tree. And then I wouldn't have my stuff."

It was true, and I knew it better than anyone. But it seemed weird for a little kid to be thinking like that. "Getting hit by a bus is pretty rare."

"Jo and my parents won't let me be entombed, though. And that's the most important part."

I pointed to the long, thin instrument used to pull brains out the nose. "Yes. Because it's weird."

"Someone's already helping with the sarcophagus and I'm working on the ceremonial speech, but I'll need anointing oils . . ."

Jo slid back into the seat. "You're not still talking about this."

Max clammed up and I felt sorry for him. For whatever reason, he seemed to think he needed an entombment party. I wasn't sure why Jo and her parents thought it was so terrible since boys could do worse things, but it wasn't any of my business.

"It was nice to see you outside of school, Grace," Jo said. "Maybe we can hang out. Or ride bikes, and I can show you around. You should see the park."

A Secret Meadow. The words from Mama's postcard came back to me. If anyone might know where it was, it would be Jo. But I had to think through what I might say. Maybe draw a bubble map of ideas that wouldn't sound so strange and pick the best one.

"Hey! Maybe you can spend the night! We can stay up and watch old movies all night and eat cheese corn. It's my favorite thing to do."

Grandma waved me over as Jo prattled on about some old actors named Cary Grant and Debra Kerr, and was it pronounced Kerr or Car, and what kind of cheese corn did I like, orange or white, and to practice taking deep breaths in preparation for the life-altering movie that was *An Affair to Remember.*

"Maybe," I said. "I'm still unpacking."

"You must have a lot of stuff," she said.

I almost laughed at that. Max gave me a salute, and I went over to meet Grandma, who was wrapping a wool scarf around her neck.

"Miranda!" Lou called from the kitchen. "Can you take a delivery down to the sheriff?"

Grandma seemed resistant as she fidgeted with her scarf, but Lou wasn't taking no for an answer. She made a beeline for us and practically shoved the bag into Grandma's arms.

They exchanged a look I couldn't figure out, then Grandma headed for the door.

"You come back, Grace. Anytime," Lou said, and handed me a paper napkin. On it, I recognized Archer's sketching from art class. Only this time it was a drawing of himself, a soup ladle in his hand like a mighty sword, the other hand pouring a glass of water over his own head. I looked around but couldn't see him anywhere.

"He's hiding," she said. "I'm sure he'll question me for the next twenty minutes about your reaction."

I tried to smooth my face so she couldn't see what I was feeling. Which I wasn't even sure about myself. My feelings were getting hard to keep straight, as they had a mind of their own. Hooligans were what they were. Hooligans running around inside, making a general mess of things so that I didn't much know if I was coming or going.

"Tell him thank you," I said as I stuffed the napkin in my pocket.

14

A Solitary Bird

Sheriff Bergum's office was one room with two jail cells at the far end, exactly like the Wild West movies I'd watched with Lacey on Movie Fridays. I half expected someone named Old Smokey to be lounging on one of the cots, drunk and singing about his mother, but the cells were empty. The cots new.

He sat at the front desk, pondering a game of Scrabble he had set up on an old-fashioned TV tray. When he saw it was Grandma, he stood up suddenly, the tray almost falling over. Once he got the tray settled, he ran a hand over his bald head like he was smoothing invisible hair.

Grandma set the soup on the desk. "I see you've been cheating again."

"I'm playing against myself. As long as we both follow the rules I make up, I figure it's fine. However, if you were to play, then I'd follow the rules to a perfect T." Sheriff Bergum laid down a series of tiles that spelled WINDORF.

"That's a type of salad, in case you were wondering. My favorite, as a matter of fact."

"I'm sure you mean Waldorf."

"Perhaps if I had some real Windorf salad, I might remember how to spell it."

My eyes drifted around the room and landed on a short file cabinet next to the desk with a single mint-colored origami crane peeking out from behind a gathering of picture frames.

As they went on and on about manure and weather and other boring nonsense, I tried to think. I wasn't crazy enough to believe Mama was leaving me treasure-hunt clues and origami directly, but I believed she was behind it somehow, the way wind will set a sail in a certain direction. The idea of Sheriff Bergum being the sail, taking the time to fold origami cranes with his sausage fingers and leave them for me, was plain unacceptable. He looked like the type of person who might need his chin to fold things.

Sheriff Bergum noticed me looking toward the picture frames and handed me one. "That's me and your grandpa when we played football together in high school. Your grandpa was the one who came up with my nickname. We were young boys when he started calling me 'Hamburger,' and 'Ham' just stuck."

"People actually call you Ham?"

"Only my friends." And then he winked at me.

He put the picture back and took another one. It looked like Mama as a teenager with Grandpa. They were both in a tree, laughing.

"Not the best way to go birding, as climbing trees tends to scare them away, but we sure had some fun."

"You used to go birding too?"

"I did. Still do. Your grandmother put in a whole section of the park for bird watchers. There's nesting boxes and feeders. We get out there with nesting materials in the spring so they can build their homes. It's a relaxing lunchtime break. You should head over with me sometime. More birds come every day."

He put the photo back and I looked over the rest of the pictures. Children. Grandchildren. An old wedding photo of a young Sheriff Bergum and a very pretty girl. I wondered if it was possible to know a person based on the pictures they surrounded themselves with.

As much as I wanted to know if this was another of Mr. Flinch's cranes, asking Sheriff Bergum didn't feel like the right thing to do. Sort of like cheating on a test. Somehow I knew Mama didn't want that. Not yet.

"Thanks for the soup, Miranda," Sheriff Bergum said. He took hold of her hand and kissed it and I had to admit he was a comfortable-looking sort of person. Like his pants didn't bind and his shirt buttons didn't pull and the leather of his belt was just the right kind of soft, which then made me wonder where in the heck he got clothes that big.

He looked my way and I stuffed my hands in my pockets.

After promising to make him a Waldorf salad, Grandma led me back to the truck.

"Do you like Sheriff Bergum?" I said.

"Of course I like him. We've been friends for years."

"No. Do you *like* like him. Because he likes you."

Grandma's fingers went all over the cross under her scarf. "Well, it certainly . . . never . . . um."

"So you do like him."

Grandma didn't answer. Instead she said, "Oh! Mrs. Greene called after you left."

"What? Why didn't you tell me earlier?" I said, stopping in the middle of the street.

"Worry tends to push things out of my mind. Then you were eating with your friends."

"They aren't my friends."

"Oh, for heaven's sake, Grace. Come out of the street."

Grudgingly, I followed her into the truck and Granny Smith started right up. Grandma pulled into the light Main Street traffic.

"Well?" I demanded. "Why didn't they answer?"

"It seems Lacey had a sleepover last night, and on the

132

way home this morning, Mrs. Greene got a flat tire and she didn't have her cell phone with her. They felt horrible for missing the call."

"A sleepover?"

"Apparently."

Lacey never had sleepovers. We only ever stayed with each other. "Did Mrs. Greene say where she had a sleepover?"

"We didn't get into details. Only that Lacey would call later."

Lacey had been at a sleepover while I was busy not sleeping in a leaky shed, scared and lonely.

Eventually Grandma came to a squeaky stop in front of the shed. "So you're not really working on the documentary with Jo."

"No."

Grandma looked disappointed. "We have to be able to trust each other, Grace."

I wasn't sure how to trust someone who might kick me out of the house if I made a big enough mistake. Then I thought about the fact that I was trying to make a big enough mistake so she would kick me out of the house, and I confused myself.

When I closed the truck door, she drove to the house, orange mud splattering. Instead of going inside the shed, I walked to the pasture fence and clicked my tongue, calling for Beauty. Her warm nose found its way into my palm, comforting, and I wished for a river-silent room with a warm bed to sleep in.

I stormed around the shed as I got my chores done, thoughts ping-ponging between Lacey's sleepover and what I'd learned about my father. More than I had ever learned from the one person who could have told me the most.

I'd always understood Mama didn't want to talk about the past because it made her so sad. But now I was starting to get mad. I'd been thrown into a job without the proper tools. Like maybe I was supposed to saw down a tree, only Mama left me with a butter knife and some wishes and dreams to work with. I should have known my father from her. She should have told me more about Grandma. She should have told me about Margery and this town and the good she must have found here so I wouldn't have to start from scratch.

Words poked at me, but I was so mad, I didn't want to reach for them, afraid I might think some foul thing that I wouldn't be able to un-think. The notion of all that made me feel sixteen different kinds of disloyal, so I tried to send my blame back toward Grandma, how none of this would be happening if it weren't for that bus ride so long ago. But it didn't work.

In a huff, I sat down on the sofa and laid out my clues to put myself in a better frame of mind: the unfinished crane from Mama's toolbox and the Threads postcard. Then I took out the stack of Daddy's flyers.

It didn't take me long to notice some had writing on the back. Typewriting. Six pages out of twenty-one.

The writing was an attempt at a poem, the pages covered in fragments and cross-outs. I could see the idea come together, the whole poem typed at the bottom of a blue flyer.

A solitary bird, hollow it flew
Through a haze of months marked by the moon
Come to a meadow, shiny with dew
Where hollow bones sang, and deep inside grew
The secret hum of a daisy in June.

And on a sixth page was a map, in what looked like Mama's careful hand, that actually said *A Secret Meadow* just like the postcard. The map had a squiggly line of river and trees and a trail that led to a meadow with tiny daisies. There weren't any landmarks. It could have been a map to anywhere. But it was a clue!

My mind tried again to put things in orderly lines. But I fought it. I wanted to float on this magic for a while. Mama would have been so proud of me.

15

Happy Detention

I didn't take Lacey's calls over the next couple of days. It wasn't logical to be mad at her for having a sleepover, but there it was.

When I got to school on Wednesday morning, Jo was waiting by the front door. "Oh my gosh, Grace! You'll never guess what I found!"

She foisted a thin manila folder into my hands.

Before I could open it, she said, "Your mom built the fountain!"

"What fountain?"

"The one in the park!"

In the folder were a few newspaper clippings. The *Sacramento Bee*. The *Union*. The *Mountain Democrat*. They all said the same thing.

> *Anna Jessup, age 16, built the fountain that will mark the center point of the Bear River Park designed by her mother, Miranda Jessup, in Auburn Valley,*

California. Miss Jessup has entitled it "Wings." An unveiling will take place on Saturday afternoon at ten o'clock in the morning, followed by a celebration at the Spoons Souperie on Main Street.

Jo was jumping up and down. "My parents had their first kiss at that fountain. So technically, I might not be here if it weren't for your mom! That almost makes us sisters!"

"Can you take me there?"

The smile fell off her face. "Right now?"

"Just tell me how to find it. I don't want you to get in trouble for ditching." I could feel Mama so strong, her hand at my back. Maybe it was that easy. The meadow could be in the park.

Jo said very seriously, "I have never ditched school in my life. As soon as we don't show up in first period, they will call your grandma and my parents, who will probably ground us for life."

"I have to do this," I said.

She picked up her backpack and slung it over one shoulder. "I've waited my whole life for something like this to happen!"

Bear River Park was a quarter mile from school down a side street and up a small hill. According to Jo, it was twenty acres. It wasn't like a normal park, with a swing set and a tree and a bunch of grass. It was like an enchanted forest. There was a wide main path lined with gravel that branched off into narrower paths, which led to a series of nooks and crannies. There was a stone bench sitting in the heart of a stand of cedars, and tire swings hung from ancient trees. There were stone bridges over creeks and a huge expanse of grass, big enough to play softball, and a gazebo off to one side. People walked arm in arm, their dogs on leashes. I saw Lou and Mel's tree house with a hand-painted sign honoring Billy's service.

The bird sanctuary Sheriff Bergum had talked about was huge, at least an acre of trees with a pond in the middle, nesting boxes all around, and birds singing for all they were worth. Several of the trees had birdhouses of all different sizes and colors on every branch. There were birdbaths made with brightly colored mosaic tiles.

I felt a sense of calm just being here. It felt like a place where Mama would have come, where I could be close to her. She said she'd never leave me, that not even death could separate us, and I saw her there in the rustle of the leaves overhead, the trickling sound of water, the rainbow-colored birdhouses.

"Is there a meadow here? Near the river or a creek?" I said.

"A meadow?"

"Someplace big and flat, where wild daisies grow?"

The puzzled look on Jo's face gave me the answer.

"Just the gazebo with the flat grassy area. But no daisies. There's music in the park on Sundays all summer long. Mrs. Snickels was married in that gazebo."

There were plaques beside each project: SPONSORED BY THE QUILTING BEE, IN MEMORY OF SPARKS, or CLASS OF 1985.

Then we came to Mama's fountain.

Trees were cleared away to give room for the sun to shine down in better weather. The sculpture in the center of the fountain was a larger version of the birds I'd seen her put together a hundred gazillion times. The walls of the fountain were made of white granite, short enough to sit on. Piles of coins both shiny and dull rested on the bottom. A pipe, maybe eight feet long, came up through the center and pumped water onto a cascade of wings and rusted feathers, all cut from metal.

Mama's plaque read:

Where the bird was before it flew,
Where the flower was before it grew,
Where bird and flower were one and the same.

The lines were from one of Frost's poems, "In a Vale." On the nights Mama ended her reading with that poem, I knew we'd be moving soon. It was a leaving sort of poem, or at least that was always what it felt like to me. I wondered why Mama had picked those lines for her fountain.

"I come here all the time when it gets warm and film the wildlife, which includes people," Jo said. "It's my very favorite place to be, except on my horse. The flowers are just starting to come up now. But in the next couple of weeks, it will look like heaven."

"Your grandma spends so much time out here, clipping and planting and moving things from one place to another. You can tell how much she loves it here."

Once again my feelings about Grandma were tripping over themselves and landing in a heap. I couldn't fit the Grandma I'd fixed in my mind with someone who could create a place like this.

"When does she come? She's always at home, with me."

"She comes during the day while we're at school. My mom and other people in town come out to help from time to time. It's like everyone's backyard."

Suddenly I understood why Grandma was always wearing her gardening uniform, why she brought her gardening tools into the truck when she drove me to school. She was on her way to tend the park.

Jo looked at the fountain. "She won't ever talk about it, though. She won't give me an interview for my documentary."

"Some people aren't talkers," I said.

"But she's the heart of the story."

I sat on the edge of the fountain and touched the freezing-cold water, thinking about Grandma being the heart of something. A couple jogged by with their Chihuahua, his tiny legs barely keeping up. They both looked our way with a puzzled expression. It was a school day, after all.

"How well do you know her?" I said.

Jo sat next to me and wiped the bottom of one boot in the grass. She took her video camera out of her backpack and fidgeted with it. "I've known her my whole life."

"What's she like?"

"Keeps to herself, mostly. Mom has me run over jams and cookies when she bakes or cans. Mrs. Jessup always asks me inside and makes me a cup of tea. She listens to me go on and on about stuff sometimes. She has good advice. I've always felt a little sorry for her, since she didn't seem to have any friends or family. I didn't know about you."

"Of course you didn't. Why should she mention having a granddaughter?"

"I know you're mad. But do you know what she did just before you got here? She had me and Max help her box up your mom's room because she thought you'd want it for yourself. Then she brought over these decorating magazines and we looked through them for ideas. Once she realized she didn't even know your favorite color, we all decided it would be best if you got to decorate for yourself."

On one of the days Grandma came to Mrs. Greene's before the funeral, a day I'd refused to come with her, she'd asked my favorite color. I thought it was such a stupid question at the time. Like out of all the questions in the universe, she picked that one?

The truth was, maybe I wanted to give Grandma a chance. And if I was clean honest with myself, there was some little crumb inside that had felt that way for a long time, her being my only other living family. But giving her a chance felt like a betrayal to Mama, and I didn't know how to change that inside myself. She'd only been gone twenty-six days.

Jo stood up and wiped the seat of her jeans. She pointed the camera toward the sky and turned it on, turning around in a slow circle. Then she turned it off. I looked up and saw how the tree tips formed a perfect circle of green with blue sky in the middle. It was an image I would have liked to write about in my notebook.

A perfect circle above my head
Leaves that cling to a blue-sky bed

"We should go back. We might just get the whole town

142

looking for us if we don't," Jo said as she put her camera away.

"Can I show you something first?" I took out the flyer with the map and pointed to the daisy meadow. "Do you know where that is?"

She turned the flyer this way and that. I noticed her fingernails were painted blue. "I don't. Where did you get it?"

"Found it in my mom's . . . room."

"Well, there are only so many trails that lead down to the river, if that's what these curvy lines mean. We could start with the trails."

"How many are there?"

"I don't know, seven, maybe eight? It's a small town."

"Don't tell my grandma, okay? She might . . . worry. Or something." The last thing I needed was Grandma asking a bunch of pesky questions I didn't want to answer.

"Cool. Our first secret. I'll come by on Saturday. How about after lunch?"

"Sounds good."

I smiled, and Jo reached in her pocket. She brought out two shiny pennies and gave me one.

"Here's to finding your meadow."

We stood next to the fountain and tossed our pennies. I wondered if there was a coin in there somewhere with Mama's wish. Or maybe Grandma's.

"Thanks for bringing me here," I said.

"You belong here just as much as anyone. You probably don't feel that way yet. But you will."

The sky didn't have answers, but it was a good place to look while I tried to find them inside myself.

Grandma and Mrs. Brannigan were sitting in Mr. Flinch's office when we got back to school during second period. We were in big trouble, but no one had called out the national guard or anything. They hadn't even bothered Sheriff Bergum since we were both missing and they figured we'd gone off together.

"What in the world were you thinking?" Mrs. Brannigan yelled. She had thrown a sweater over her pajamas. She still had her slippers on. Big fluffy pink slippers with glittery silver poufs on top. "With everything that's going on, you're going to ditch school and give me seven different kinds of heart attack?"

"I'm sorry, Mom," Jo said, head down.

"It's my fault," I said.

"Where did you go?" Grandma asked.

Jo looked at me for direction. Grandma sat so straight in her chair, and it finally clicked that she wasn't stiff; she just had good posture from being a ballerina.

"We went to the park," I said softly.

They all let out a collective breath.

"What? Did you think we ran away to join the circus?" Jo said.

"Of course not," Mr. Flinch said, tugging at the purple sleeves of his sweater. "However, we did call over to Lafollette's to make sure no one bought a bus ticket. Mrs. Miller informed me there was no way she'd ever sell a bus ticket to a child under eighteen without a parent or guardian present, and who did we think she was? So now, on top of everything else, I have to bring Mrs. Miller a batch of brownies to smooth her ruffled feathers."

"A bus ticket? Why would we want a bus ticket?" Jo said.

The only idea these people had of me was that I might run away. Just like Mama did.

"I'm sorry to say that you will each have detention today," Mr. Flinch said. "I'm sure I can find something supremely horrible for you to do. Perhaps we can decipher some *Othello*."

Grandma stood up. "That's twice," she said to me. "Don't do it again."

Before I knew what to say, or how to feel, she opened the door to leave. But instead of slamming out, she turned around. "And you're going to help Mr. Flinch with those brownies. Then you're going to bring me some so I can have them with my tea. I could use some chocolate about now."

So instead of deciphering *Othello*, which made me think of Ginger Peppers, Mr. Flinch had us help him make brownies in the cafeteria kitchen for detention. Jo tried to do some filming, but he said it defeated the purpose of detention to let her do something she loved. Some might think we were getting off easy by baking brownies, but Mr. Flinch taught as we baked. He made us do fractions while we measured, wouldn't let us taste the batter, and then, when the first batch didn't turn out exactly right, he made us start over. And we didn't get to eat any. Not a crumb.

When we were finally done, we put a plate together for Grandma and one for Mrs. Brannigan. Then Mr. Flinch took us to hand-deliver the remaining still-warm brownies to Mrs. Miller at Lafollette's, where she promptly gave me and Jo an earful about who did we think we were, giving her and everyone else a worry attack. She was tall, almost as tall as Mr. Flinch, and wide at the shoulders. She gave me a bear hug that squeezed the air out of my lungs, and then she gave one to Jo. Once we'd been sufficiently squeezed, we eyeballed the brownies. Mrs. Miller took a big bite and offered one to Mr. Flinch. Then she tucked the plastic back around the paper plate and put them away. "Happy detention, ladies."

16

A Secret
Meadow

Dear Grace,

Okay. So this is the last regular letter I'm going to send. If you won't take my calls, I'm going to start sending you every terrible poem I write until you can't stand it anymore.

You're smiling right now, I can feel it.

So, I wasn't there when you needed me. I'm sure you feel pretty crappy about it. Otherwise, you'd be taking my calls by now. But you have to understand that I loved your mama too, and now my best friend is gone. I've been a wreck. I know you don't want to hear that because you've probably been a worse wreck, and you have a better reason for it. I've been such a mess, in fact, that Marsha Trett isn't making fun of me even though she loves that more than chocolate chip cookies. And we all know how much she loves those.

So Jill and Carrie felt sorry for me and told me I had two choices. 1) I could spend the night at Jill's *house, where we wouldn't do anything monumental and we wouldn't watch any movies like* My Girl *or* Shiloh *or anything that might cause endless amounts of sobbing. We would make stupid faces at each other anytime the mood got the slightest bit blue. I'm talking summer-sky-almost-white blue. And anytime I got that hound-dog look on my face, they had permission to put an ice cube down the back of my shirt and hold it there. Or, 2) They would kill me.*

I'm sad that I missed your call, but we would have been home in time if it wasn't for Mom's stupid bald tire blowing up on the freeway.

Don't even get me started on THAT.

Here's my latest poem so you see what you will be in for.

Lint

Tiny, hairy
Scant, yet scary.
Where have you come from, O lint?
Sticky like glue
Give me a clue!
Where have you come from, O lint?
Dogs or chickens?
Fingerly pickens?

Where have you come from, O lint?
What does it matter?
Tastes like cake batter.
Now's a good time for a mint.

Love (see that? LOVE),
Lacey

When I woke up on Saturday morning, I got a fire going in the stove, set Mama's quilt in front of it, said good morning to Beauty with a pat on the nose and a carrot for her belly, and then called Lacey. I didn't understand why she hadn't brought it up in her letters I'd gotten from her every single day this week. She'd apologized for missing my call over and over again, begged and pleaded for me to call her back and generally wrote about everything but Mama and the signs. Maybe it was the sort of thing you had to talk about in person. Anyway, I couldn't wait to talk to her about the new things I'd found, like the poem and my dad, and where it all might lead. If anyone could help me figure it out, it would be Lacey.

Grandma let me call from Grandpa's office. I sat at the big desk, which smelled like furniture polish, brought the old green phone toward me, twisting the rubber cord around one finger, and dialed Mrs. Greene.

"Finally," Lacey said when she picked up the phone.

"It was the threat of bad poetry that did it."

She laughed, but it was a held-back sort of laugh.

We talked about dumb stuff. She couldn't help but gossip about Denny and Marsha, even though she swore she'd never talk about him again. She talked about the upcoming dance and that she didn't have a decent dress. How Mrs. Greene was all in a lather because she'd always made Lacey's fancy dresses and now Lacey wanted one from the mall.

By the time she took a breath, I was pretty sure she was avoiding the subject of Mama and the signs on purpose.

"Did you get the letter I sent last week?" I said.

"Yes," she said, hesitant.

"Well, I think I found the next clue in my treasure hunt," I said. "I went to Threads and the lady there knew my father. She gave me these flyers that he'd collected and there was a poem on one of them and a map on another. I'm sure Mama must have written the poem, and the map has *A Secret Meadow* written on it. With daisies. Remember what Mama used to say about daisies?"

It was quiet on the other end. "Lacey?"

"I'm here."

"Well, what do you think?"

"It's just a little . . . out there."

The thought made me panic. "Maybe not. Maybe you get some kind of extra powers in heaven, or there's a tiny part of you that gets left behind, or . . ."

"Dying doesn't make you a superhero."

"How do you know?" I said.

"I guess I don't. But if it were true, it would be a miracle. And miracles don't happen to just anybody. They happen to, I don't know, Olympic teams or something."

There wasn't much to say after that. I listened to her go on for a while about what color dress she might get and was there anyone interesting here and was I still working on Plan B to get myself back home.

I assured her that I was and we hung up. I closed my eyes and tried to quiet the thoughts rushing through my head, but they wouldn't still, so I pretended I had my notebook and pencil and after a while my thoughts worked themselves into orderly lines.

A whole school year.
Start to finish.
Long enough to know
quirks,
facial expressions
and tones of voice,
mine and hers.
I had to get back
while the faded lines of me
were still there enough
to trace

back

into place.

I tried to put Lacey's doubts out of my head as I went to have breakfast with Grandma. Jo was coming by in a couple of hours so we could start our official search for the Secret Meadow, and once I found more clues, there was no way Lacey could keep being such a skeptic.

But the hunt wasn't just about the clues and finding my way home. It was about this growing feeling that I'd be closer to Mama at Mrs. Greene's since that was where she died, and that somehow, she might just be there on the porch waiting for me if only for one shimmering moment.

There were two mugs next to Grandma on the counter. One said LAKE ALMANOR and the other said DAD. I felt a small pang of guilt that I was trying so hard to get back to Mrs. Greene's, but figured I could get to know Grandma from there. Decide how much of a chance she deserved.

I took Lake Almanor. The mug had a drawing of a teardrop-shaped lake with pine trees dotting the sides and oversized fish swimming its depths. "Where's that?" I said as I popped down a piece of bread in the toaster. I so much wanted to talk about Lacey and how bad I felt, that I almost said something to Grandma, but I caught myself.

Grandma wiped down the counter where she'd spilled

some water. "Up north. We fished and went birding there every summer. Stayed in these cute little cabins. Kokanee Lodge, it was called."

"Mama liked to fish?" I couldn't picture it.

"When she was a little girl. Once she turned eight, though, she refused to hook the worms and she and your grandpa turned to birding instead."

"Why didn't you go with them?"

"I'm not one for sitting and waiting for things to happen." She touched the cross at her neck. "Besides, someone had to keep their feet on the ground while those two went flying off."

There was the smallest hint of irritation in her voice. It was exactly the way I'd felt about Mama sometimes. How she always left me thinking about the hard things, the boring things. The sturdy and practical things. I dug my toes into the hooked rug and changed the subject.

"Why don't you have any pictures out?" I said.

"I put them in the attic years ago."

"Why?"

She looked stumped for a second, like she'd never thought to ask herself that question. "They were hard to look at," she said.

"Seems to me the empty walls would be worse," I said.

Grandma gave me a long look and then set her mug in the sink. "Come on," she said. She walked out of the kitchen without waiting, her footsteps thumping down the hall and up the stairs. As I quickly buttered my toast, I heard a loud coiled *snap* come from the upstairs landing. The house creaked. Then silence.

I munched my toast as I walked up the stairs. The ladder to the attic had been pulled down from the ceiling, but I couldn't hear so much as a rustle of paper.

Then I heard a heavy *thud*.

A lightning bolt of panic. "Grandma?"

Nothing.

I took the rest of the creaky wooden steps two at a time and stood at the bottom of the attic ladder.

"Grandma?"

"Up here." Grandma's voice was thin, miles away.

I grabbed hold of the ladder and climbed hand over hand. There were several unlit bulbs hanging along a wood beam in the center of the attic. Grandma slouched over some boxes in a pool of light from the attic dormer. Dust swirled around her head like a halo.

I knocked my shins on boxes and crates trying to get across the room to crouch beside her.

"What is it?" I said, afraid she might be having a heart attack or some other kind of attack and that I'd have to zoom back out to get to the phone.

Her face was pained and she had one hand over her heart, panicking me even more. "They're ruined," she said.

That's when I noticed several pictures spread across the floor, splotched and destroyed by water. The boxes were a soggy mess. The roof must have been leaking for a while.

She closed her eyes and sat perfectly still. I raised my hand toward her shoulder, then pulled it back.

"They can't all be gone," I said, as much for myself as for her.

Grandma opened her eyes. I looked for moisture, but they were bone-dry. Could be an old-person condition, I supposed. Could be that some old people dried out little by little until they blew away.

"I need to get Mr. Brannigan to look at this roof." Grandma pushed her hands against her knees for support as she tried to hoist herself to her feet. Her knees had other ideas. It took two more tries.

I picked up a soggy box. She picked up another.

We spent an hour going through the pictures at the breakfast table, silently, side by side, separating the ruined ones from the ones that made it. I felt my hard edges toward her soften as she brushed a tear away from her cheek from time to time. I must have been wrong about her drying out.

"I've been there!" I said, grabbing a picture of Mama as a small girl sitting on a bench with a park behind her.

Grandma took the picture and looked it over. "I designed that park. It's in Sacramento."

"We went there all the time after we moved in with Mrs. Greene. Mama liked to walk the trails."

We sat there in the silence of what it might mean. And then I realized, really and fully realized, that I would never know. So many things, I would never know.

I thought about how long it might take to have Jo help me find the meadow. How even though Auburn Valley was a small town, the meadow could be anywhere along the river. Or a creek, which I hadn't thought of until I saw Grandma's park. The longer it took me to follow the clues, the longer it would take me to get back to Mrs. Greene and Lacey.

Even though I wasn't ready to tell Grandma much of anything, I was desperate, so I took the flyer with the map out of my pocket and handed it to her.

After looking it over for a few seconds, she said, "This is a map to your mama's meadow. She and your grandpa swore it had some kind of magical power that called the birds. He said if they told people, they might come steal the magic, so they kept it secret."

"Can you take me?"

"Get your coat," Grandma said. And we were off.

Just like that.

17

Wheel of Fortune

As Grandma led me through the garden, Beauty came up to the fence and gave us a good-natured grunt.

"I don't have any carrots for you," Grandma said, and Beauty grunted again.

"I'll bring some later!" I called.

The garden led to a path I hadn't seen on my one and only trip through these woods from that first day, which seemed so long ago. The path curved and then ran alongside the river, about ten feet above it, a wide, rocky slope in between. I realized I had one hand clenched into a fist as we walked. It helped, so I left it that way.

We crossed a fast-running stream that came from above and flowed on down into the river, stepping from one enormous flat stone to the next.

"Your grandpa laid these in so we could always get across."

"Tell me about him," I said.

Grandma thought for a minute, looking up into the

leafy trees. "He smoked a pipe because he thought it made him look smart." She smiled her crinkle-nosed smile. "He was a whiz with his hands, could fix anything you put in front of him. He was that way with puzzles too." We reached a curve in the trail and she paused, looking down where the river rushed by. "He was never indoors if he could be outside. I used to think he liked to garden, but he had no eye for it, so after years of watching him pull perfectly good plants and leave the weeds, I realized he just liked to be useful. But he could name every tree in the forest. He always had a book in his hand and a smile on his face." She shook her head. She went back to walking, turning to see if I was coming along. "Your mama was everything to him."

Like with Daddy, I'd made up stories about Grandpa too. From the one picture I'd seen, he didn't seem like the kind of man who wore a suit to work and said things like "quarterly reports" or "credit application." I liked to think that he was a writer, like me, or did something heroic like move cattle across the plains or build hearing aids. And now I found out my ideas of him were not all that wrong.

I let myself imagine him. The white and brown stubble of his chin. How he would smell of pipe tobacco and pine. How he would have taken my hand and walked me through the trees, pointing to this one or that, giving their proper names, like maple or ash or sycamore.

I felt a deep, burning anger at Mama. At her need to move from place to place and drag me with her. Then disloyalty slithered its squeezy fingers around my insides.

Matching breaths to the beat of my footfalls helped the squeezy feeling pass, and eventually, we came to a green meadow where I could feel the warm weather hiding just around the corner. The meadow touched the edge of a large rocky beach, the river beyond. Then I had to take calming breaths all over again as the day Mama died tried to play itself out in my mind. I shook my head and turned away from the river. I had a job to do.

There were no daisies that I could see, but I could tell this was the place where the picture of Mama and Daddy was taken. I'd stared at that picture for hours and I knew every little nook and cranny of it. The trees, although bigger, grew in the same formations. Although you couldn't see the river in the photo, you could see the edge of the rocky beach and the hills beyond, their peaks coming together in the shape of a jagged heart.

"She loved it here," Grandma said.

In the shade of the trees at the far end of the meadow was a metal sculpture. A crane. It was surrounded by a circle of white river rocks. It had long pipe legs and a ski-pole neck. The wings were made out of spoons, hundreds of them, layered like feathers.

"There's a crane reserve not far, down in Woodbridge," Grandma said. "Once in a great while, a crane or two would rest here by the river during their migration. Your grandpa told her they were magic, and if you wished on a crane, it would always come true. She believed it for a long time."

There'd been two sandhill cranes perched on the bank as I sat with Mama the morning she died. So still in the dull morning light. I knew they were sandhills because Mama had pointed them out a few weeks before she'd died, telling me how they were migrating home. I remembered thinking we'd finally found ours.

I walked up to the metal crane and brushed my hand along the spoons. I looked it over from beak to tail feathers, and down in the blown leaves, tucked up against the crane's leg, was another spoon, like the ones used as feathers. I picked it up.

"Your mama used to take those spoons from Lou and Mel. She put them in every one of her pieces. Lou took such pride in the fact that her spoons were such a big part of your mama's art."

Maybe the next place to look for a clue was Spoons. I laid my ear against the crane's belly. "Did Mama put something inside?"

"I'm not sure. She built it in your grandfather's work-shop and wouldn't let me see until it was time to haul it into the meadow. I always thought it was her penance, her way of saying she was sorry. Then I went ahead and sent her off anyway."

"But it wasn't her fault."

"No, it wasn't."

I walked to the edge of the meadow and watched the river, sinking down to my knees. I plucked a blade of long grass and stared at it, hard, willing myself not to cry.

They'd told me Mama had fallen down and knocked her head before rolling into the water to drown. Just like that. Because I'd been so mad at her about wanting to leave, I didn't let her climb into bed with me that night to read Robert Frost. So she went walking instead.

"You found her," Grandma said, coming up behind me.

"I don't want to talk about it."

"Are you sure?"

Grandma kneeled beside me and I wished for a pair of her gardening knee pads so my knees wouldn't get wet and muddy from the grass.

Her hands were right there. Sitting on her lap. I wanted her to take mine and tell me everything would be okay. In this one moment, I might have believed her.

But then the moment passed and I was stuck with the river again. It started to sprinkle.

"Your mama never told you about what happened here, did she? What led to her bus trip to Texas."

I shook my head, not sure I wanted to know, at the same time not sure I wanted to keep myself from knowing certain things anymore. Because even though Mama had told me about Grandma and why she didn't go home, I always knew there was something else. Some Deep Thing she kept hidden the same way I hid Grandma's letters and my secret wish to stay in one place long enough to see the seasons turn.

"No," I said.

Grandma stood up with her creaky knees and I stood up with her. "I was angry," she said. "I had no right to it, but by the time I figured that out, your mama was long gone. I kept waiting to hear from her. I honestly thought she'd come home. And then the months stretched into years and I got angry all over again."

"Why were you angry to begin with?"

Grandma didn't seem to know what to say. "Because your mother lived and your grandfather died, I suppose. As horrible as that is."

It took me a minute to put things together. "She was in the car with Grandpa and my dad?"

Grandma nodded. "They were running away. Your mama and Scott." She picked at a callus on her palm.

"There was a big snowstorm that day and things had been tense. When your mama went to bed early, your grandpa had a bad feeling about it. Sure enough, he checked and found her gone, a note saying they were leaving. I tried to tell your grandpa they couldn't get anywhere in the storm, but he wasn't having any of it. He took off and found them huddled under the awning at Lafollette's. Margery had gotten them there. Somehow, Thomas must have talked them into coming home, and then the car went off the road."

Grandma cleared her throat. "Both your father and grandfather were killed instantly. Your mother didn't have a scratch."

Those last words were shaped with blame.

I remembered how Mama and I had watched *Wheel of Fortune* on her nights off. How we'd crack up because we could never figure out the words on the board. A contestant would call out something like *"The Bridge on the River Kwai!"* and we'd crack up some more because who could pull *"The Bridge on the River Kwai"* out of a few random consonants? Then Vanna White would turn the rest of the letters and, sure enough, we'd see it for ourselves, clear as day.

Mama had always been like a *Wheel of Fortune* board with only half the letters turned. Now that Grandma turned the rest of them for me, I saw everything. Why Mama didn't talk about her past. Why she always had that little crease between her eyes, even when she laughed. Why she didn't settle anywhere. Like there was some purpose in being uncomfortable.

"Why were they running away?"

But I knew, of course. I'd always known, even if I never wanted to think about it. It was because of me. Mama was pregnant with me and she was only seventeen.

"We felt she needed time away from Scott. That she had some considering to do . . . about her future."

"You wanted Mama to give me up."

When I said it, I didn't know if it was true or not, but the fact that Grandma couldn't meet my eyes gave me all the answer I needed.

In a flash, a whole other life washed over me. The life I could have had if Grandma had been the type of mother who loved her daughter through a hard time. If she'd accepted the fact that I was coming, that Mama and Daddy loved each other even though they were young. Then I would have been born here, in this town, with a mother and father, a grandma and grandpa. I wouldn't be coming twelve years late, trying to carve out a place for myself one more time.

A fury came over me thinking I'd almost trusted her.

"If you would have just loved her, loved me, they never would have tried to run away. No one would be dead."

I didn't wait for her to answer. I ran out of the meadow and down the trail, sending birds into the sky as I went.

18

Too Precious
to Throw Away

Mama wouldn't start a new project until she had every piece. Sometimes it took months of gathering. We'd go to yard sales and junk shops and she'd let her hands run along rows of knobs and buttons and screws that had held other people's lives together in one form or fashion for more years than I'd been alive. She let herself imagine those lives, what kind of bird she might piece together. One time I asked her how she knew what to pick and what to leave behind. She said the right pieces hummed under her hand, like the daisies. I remembered sitting in the tub night after night, for a long time, humming, so she knew not to leave me behind. Then she went ahead and did it anyway.

The trick was figuring out what to take and what to leave behind. Moving so many times, we should have had it down to a science, but Mama wasn't one for science or anything else that might require making lists and putting things in proper order. She'd throw this or that into the boxes we kept with us always, the ones that fit perfectly in Daisy's hatchback, and that was that. From one move to the next, there were additions and subtractions based on Mama's art, what she might need for her birds. Once she'd left behind our bedding because she needed the space for a bunch of old watering cans and a box of hand-painted tiles she'd collected. Bedding was easy to replace.

But I always felt a sadness for those things that were left, like they had proper feelings or something. Being left behind was like a shadow that never went away.

Unlike Mama's boxes, my canvas duffel always had the same stuff. Clothes. The photo album. A needlepoint pillow that I'd made with our landlord in Hanford, Mrs. Smithson, when I was six. There was a pack of strawberry seeds from kindergarten, a small bag of beach sand, a few more odds and ends. At the very bottom was the packet of unsent letters I'd written to Grandma when I was eight years old.

She banged on the shed door. "Grace, let me in. We need to talk about this."

"Go away!"

"I will not go away. I will stand here in the rain until you open this door."

Leave it to Grandma to ruin my plan. I opened the door a crack. "I'm sorry for yelling at you. I'm tired. I just want to take a nap. Can we please talk about this later?"

Grandma narrowed her eyes, skeptical, and tried to look around me and into the shed. "Are you sure?" she finally said.

I nodded and then closed the door, leaning against it until I heard her boots squishing through the mud back up the trail.

Once she was good and gone, I took her letters out of my duffel and threw them across the shed. I made sure all my cranes and things were in the Kerr jar, along with Mama's bird poem. *A solitary bird, hollow it flew.* It was as though she'd written it for me.

Whatever didn't fit in the duffel, I packed into Mama's toolbox. Daddy's book of Robert Frost poems, all the extra flyers, and Archer's Ladle Boy picture.

I curled up in my sleeping bag and pulled Mama's quilt around my shoulders. When Jo knocked at the door some time later that afternoon to try and find the meadow, I ignored her. She knocked a few more times, calling my name, but I just shoved the pillow over my head and waited for it to get dark.

I pushed Mummy Max and Jo out of my mind. I tried not to think of Beauty and what her baby might look like. Then I pushed away the meadow, and the fact that Mama's next clue was probably the spoons that made up the crane's wings. It was just the sort of clever thing she'd expect me to pick up. Since I was sure she was eventually leading me to Mrs. Greene's anyway, I supposed it didn't really matter.

I didn't worry as I climbed in the car because Mama had taught me how to drive when I was nine, declaring that if there were ever an emergency and she keeled over in the middle of nowhere, she wasn't about to have me starving to death because I hadn't learned such a simple thing as driving. Just before I turned the ignition, I said a little prayer that starting Daisy wouldn't wake this half of the mountainside.

But I didn't need the prayer. She was quiet, as though she might understand my need for it, and I drove off that mountain and down through the darkened windows of town, thinking I should have done this sooner. After I was good and far away, I pulled over and took Mama's map of California out of my duffel, the pinholes reminding me of where I'd been. Mama had always put up the map before we'd leave a place, pacing back and forth in front of it for a good week or so. She'd go to the library and research towns with lakes or hills or what have you, or she'd pick a random city newspaper online and read the For Rent listings. When she was satisfied with her newly discovered town, she'd thumbtack it on the map, and off we'd go.

Once we'd gotten to Mrs. Greene's, even Mama had said it was where we were supposed to be. We'd found her house because we'd been driving around, going to garage and yard sales, and drove right by Mrs. Greene's big old farmhouse with this giant plastic pink flamingo mailbox in the front yard, which Mama took as a signpost.

They didn't even have a For Rent sign in front of the house, but Mama knocked on the door and said this crazy thing anyway. "I think we're supposed to be here."

Instead of shying away like we were a couple of loons, Mrs. Greene got this ginormous smile and invited us in for tea and cookies.

It turned out Mrs. Greene was just finishing up this little one-bedroom cottage in the back of her property that she'd always used for storage and was about to list it for rent. Mama wrote her a deposit check that day, asked her to wait to cash it until the next Friday, when she got paid, and we were off and moving again, but this time I didn't mind. Even that first day, meeting Lacey and Mrs. Greene, I felt things would be different. Mrs. Greene didn't mind her own business, always putting her two cents in, even going as far as to chastise Mama for dragging me around to kingdom come, and for not living up to her God-given potential. I worried that might drive Mama away, but it seemed to draw her closer. She ate up what Mrs. Greene said like Snickerdoodles. So did I. "Grace, you sign up for school politics. You hear? You can think something through like nobody's business, and always come up on the logical side of things." It felt like she was giving me the wide-open world in a way Mama hadn't. I was convinced that Mrs. Greene and Lacey were the missing pieces of our family and it didn't matter one lick that we weren't related by blood. After all that moving, we'd finally found them, and I wasn't about to give them up.

I turned on the overhead light in the car as it started to rain, and found where I was on the map, tracing a line to the nearest pinhole. It was a straight shot down Highway 80 to the 193, past Sacramento, and on to Hood and Mrs. Greene. I knew how to get to Mrs. Greene's from there.

As I put the car in drive and wiped at my eyes, headlights came up behind me. They were coming fast, so I waited to let them pass. Instead, they slowed. Blue and red lights flashed, a *bleep* of siren coming next.

I rested my head against the steering wheel. Eventually, a gloved knuckle knocked on the window. Sheriff Bergum. When I didn't move to open the door, he did it for me.

"What in the world?" he demanded. He was wearing regular clothes, boots, and a plastic cover over his cowboy hat. When I didn't answer, he took hold of my elbow and helped me out. The rain came down hard. I was soaked through in seconds.

Without another word, Sheriff Bergum loaded me

into the back of his squad car and we were off in a swirl of lights.

Sheriff Bergum drove through town, with me in the back like a criminal. Maybe I was. It couldn't be legal to drive a car at twelve. Even in an emergency. I wondered if he was arresting me. If they'd send me away on a bus to someone I didn't know, like Grandma did to Mama. I wondered if I cared. That last pinball thought bounced around my head and couldn't find an answer. Not even a measly one worth five points. I was smack out of energy and my shoes were wet.

Sheriff Bergum led me into the station, turning on lights as he went, and walked me into the back cell, past the little origami crane perched behind the family photo, and sat me down. Then he actually took out a giant set of old-fashioned keys and locked me in.

"Are you kidding?" I said, unbelieving.

Even though it had been covered with a hat, his bald head was a little drippy and he took a handkerchief out of his pocket and wiped it down, like a table. Then he put his hat back on.

"Do you have any idea what you've done to your grandma? And me! I was just sitting down to watch the news and have my hot cocoa when your grandma called, frantic." He went to the phone and dialed. After murmuring for a while, he hung up with a bang.

"Can't you just take me back to her house?"

"No. She'll be here in a few minutes."

"How did she even know where I went?"

"She went out to check on you again and found you and the car gone. She called me in a panic."

With that, he hung up his plaid jacket and sat at his multidrawered desk with his back to me. Every few minutes he'd take off his cowboy hat and run a giant hand over his bald head, then put his hat back on with a *humph*. He turned to his Scrabble game.

"Can I ask you something?"

He grunted.

"Did you make that crane?" If they were going to send me away, I at least had to know where it came from.

He turned and looked at me as though I had asked the dumbest question in the history of dumb questions. "You've got bigger things to worry about," he said.

"I have to know."

Maybe it was the desperation in my voice that made him answer. Maybe it was the fact that I was shivering and my wet hair and clothes had dripped into a puddle at my feet.

He took a deep, lumbering breath, reached into the

drawer behind his desk, and took out a large wool blanket. It was exactly the same as the one they'd wrapped me in the morning Mama died. He held it through the bars. I shook my head.

"Fine." He looked at the crane. "I don't know who made it. I found it beside my front left tire after a particularly bad day at work. Some things are too precious to throw away. But you wouldn't know about that."

Sheriff Bergum knocked back a container of Tums and pointed a thick finger at me. "No more talking. You sit there and think."

Fifteen minutes later, Grandma showed up with my duffel, wearing her usual prune face and lumberjack costume. I was glad when she did. I was tired of watching Sheriff Bergum huff and puff and mumble to himself about my ingratitude and general twelve-year-old nincompoopery as though I wasn't right there listening.

"Let her on out," Grandma said.

"You should leave her. She might see things different in the morning," Sheriff Bergum said.

"I have a better idea." Grandma eyeballed me up and down. Past experience with authority figures had told me that eyeballing never amounted to anything good.

"So I'm not arrested?" I said as Sheriff Bergum let me out.

He narrowed his eyes. "You're lucky your grandma has some influence over me."

Fine. I just wanted to get out of my wet shoes and into bed anyway, where maybe I could sleep for a change.

Grandma had other plans.

19

Flat
Sure

"**Where are we going?**" I said, panicked, as we passed Daisy on the side of the road. "You aren't going to leave her there, are you?"

"I'll take care of it."

We drove deeper into the darkness and silence. Maybe this was it. She really was driving me to the bus station in Colfax since Lafollette's was closed.

It wasn't until Grandma turned onto Highway 80 and headed west that I knew where she was going. I expected relief. For some strange reason, there wasn't any.

After an hour, we came to Exit 116, California 193. Grandma made all the right turns like she knew them by heart. It was still raining, the windshield wipers a squeaking blur. She parked in front of Mrs. Greene's house and the porch light clicked on. Mrs. Greene pushed through the screen to stand there in her powder-blue robe.

"Your mother and I didn't get along, Grace. Just as she told you. Especially after the accident. I did ship her off, to my cousin in Texas, but she never made it there. I could tell you I sent her away because I felt that would be easiest on her, instead of having to live in such a small town, pregnant, after such a tragedy. But really, it was easiest for me."

I didn't know what to say. She cleared her throat.

"There isn't a day goes by that I don't blame myself for what happened. I was hard, and that set things off. I missed out on your life. On her life. For that, I have regret. I'd do things different now. I'm not sure how much that is worth to you. But it's all I have."

"You're not doing much different," I said, looking at Mrs. Greene standing in her doorway. "Considering where we are."

Grandma's face glowed a soft green from the dash lights. A tear rolled down her cheek and she brushed it away. "Sometimes you need to see where you've been so you can decide where you're going. I'll be back to pick you up in two days—Monday afternoon."

I was surprised to see the tear, but there wasn't anything else to say, so I climbed out and grabbed my duffel. I ran through the rain, and Mrs. Greene took me into her open arms, not caring one lick about my dripping hair or coat. Something I was flat sure Grandma would never do.

20

A Trick
of the Light

If you stare at something long enough and then
close your eyes, you can see the outline of it there on the
backs of your eyelids. That was how it was for me in Mrs.
Greene's house. Mama was everywhere. But only that
outline impression of her. A trick of the light I couldn't
turn into anything else.

I saw her standing beside Mrs. Greene, drying the
dishes and bumping hips. I saw Mrs. Greene put an arm
around her shoulder and kiss her right on the temple, telling her she didn't know how she got along before we came.
We filled the house with laughter and tears and all manner
of chaos, but it was the happiest chaos she'd known. Mrs.
Greene was older than Mama so she was a mother to all
of us.

As I watched her put together her special-occasion
French toast with apples and cinnamon—Mama's shadow
beside her—I got to thinking about her love of cooking
and how that had to be one of the reasons Mama and I had

stayed those nine months. After keeping grocery money in a coffee can my whole life and just buying staples—mac and cheese, hot dogs, hamburger, Wonder Bread—Mrs. Greene's fried chicken, black-eyed peas, and corn bread or her teriyaki flank steak and roasted potatoes were just what we needed. It got to the point that Mama and I stopped cooking for ourselves altogether. We shopped, Mrs. Greene cooked, and then we did dessert. It was a good system and I never knew how soothing it could be to gather around a table at the same time every day and eat good food. And laugh. With Mrs. Greene and Lacey, we laughed a lot.

Mrs. Greene swooped in with two plates heaped with French toast and set them down in front of me and Lacey. Then she brought over a plate of bacon while Lacey talked about Denny Thompson, whom we'd both had a crush on what felt like a lifetime ago, and now he was in love with Marsha Trett. Mrs. Greene rotated between tsking, ooh-ing and ahhing, and saying, "Lordy!" or, "What nerve!" depending on what was needed in the moment.

"He likes her because of her bra size." Lacey whispered the last two words as though saying them any louder might singe her eyebrows. "And is she decent enough to be insulted? Nope. She goes around smoothing her shirt and posing this way and that like she has something to be proud of. Plus she eats meat."

"I eat meat. So do you," I said around a mouthful of bacon.

"Yes, but we haven't eaten beef tongue."

"No, sir," Mrs. Greene said. "And I never will."

I remembered the day it came up. We were playing truth or dare at lunch recess, and when Marsha picked truth, Lacey asked her what was the grossest thing she'd ever eaten and liked. When Marsha said beef tongue, Lacey never recovered.

"I noticed you aren't carrying around your notebook. I used to think it was stuck to your armpit," Mrs. Greene said.

It was too confusing to explain my thoughts on Before and After, since I wasn't real firm on it myself. "I haven't much felt like writing."

"I don't much feel like taking my fiber in the morning. But I need it."

When Mrs. Greene stood up to rinse the dishes, Lacey tapped me on the shoulder and leaned in to whisper, "C'mon." I could smell her apricot shampoo as a curl brushed my cheek.

I followed her up the stairs to Mrs. Greene's flower-patterned bedroom, where she tiptoed to the tall dresser and opened the bottom drawer, pulling out an armful of underthings. We slipped back through the hall into her room, closing the door behind us.

For the next half hour, we tried on Mrs. Greene's bras over our shirts, stuffing them with socks, lots of socks, and paraded around the room, saying, "My name is Marsha Trett, don't I look maaaaahvelous?" and then collapsing onto the floor in fits of giggles. It felt good to giggle again.

"I have a real bra," I said, feeling the wood floor solid against my back.

Lacey sat up straight. "What do you mean?"

"A real bra with an underwire and lace and stuff." I showed her. Lacey was impressed, and it was hard to impress Lacey. She stood up in front of her floor-length mirror and ran her hands over her waist and hips.

"I don't have any curves," she said with a pout.

"That's because you're a ballerina."

She stood up taller at that. "You always know just what to say, Grace. It's been awful without you. You're like my very own cheerleading section."

"You don't need me for that."

She did a fancy pirouette over to the bed and slid into one of Mrs. Greene's slips. "You must be so glad to be away from your grandma. Does she ever even smile?"

"She needs a good reason is all."

"You're sticking up for her!" she said, hands on hips.

"No, I'm not!"

"Yes, you are."

She was right. I was. Which was weird. It felt like a

reflex almost, the way you might reach up to block a ball aimed at your head before you even know what you're doing.

"I'm not sure she's as terrible as I thought," I offered.

"Is that why you've been doing dumb stuff like tracking mud in the house and unscrewing lightbulbs instead of flushing your shoes down the toilet or digging up her garden? Because your idea of sabotage is pretty lame."

I shrugged. "I'm not good at sabotage."

"Whatever."

"Are you mad about something?"

"I just don't think you're trying very hard to get back here."

"Of course I am!"

But as we cleaned up the mess of slips and underthings and put them back into Mrs. Greene's drawers, I wondered if she was right. Lacey fluffed her hair in the mirror, twisting curls around her finger so they took their proper shape. I picked at a loose thread on her bedspread.

"I found another clue," I said.

She stopped fluffing. "Grace, seriously?"

"Why can't you just believe me?"

She tried not to look impatient. "You want me to believe your mother is sending you signs. That doesn't sound crazy to you?"

I knew it was a lot to ask. And I didn't have proof.

But I felt you should be able to talk to your best friend about anything and they should believe you, no matter what.

"Have you made any friends yet?" she said, changing the subject. Her words were snippy. Something I'd already forgotten about her in my short time away. How she could get to Snippy Town in no time flat.

Jo came to mind. How she'd offered to help me investigate the river trails without thinking it was strange or a waste of time. Max and his bandages. Archer and Ladle Boy. "There's a horse," I said.

Lacey looked mystified. "A horse?"

"Next door. She comes and visits me at the fence."

She narrowed her eyes and crossed her arms. Even a horse could make her jealous. "Jill and Carrie ask me to eat lunch with them every day, but I leave early to help Mrs. Flute with the kindergartners just like we always did. I'm suffering for you."

"So I guess suffering includes sleepovers with Jill and Carrie?"

"I already told you, they didn't give me a choice." Lacey threw herself onto the bed face-first. I twirled a lock of her hair around my finger.

"You don't need to suffer for me, Lace. I don't know how long it might take for everyone to figure out I should be here."

She popped up onto one elbow. "Promise you'll keep trying, though? No matter what?"

"Promise," I whispered.

We crossed our pinkies and the deal was sealed.

Later that afternoon, Lacey went to Denny's house to pick up a book she'd left there accidentally on purpose. I stood on the back porch for a long time and looked toward the river gliding by quietly in the distance, wondering if the footprints were all still there in the sand or if the wind and rain had washed them down to random hills and valleys. I could almost hear the static pop of the two-way radio on the police officer's belt as she sat across from me in Mrs. Greene's house with her little notebook and pen, waiting for me to say something she could write down. All I offered was, "I found her. She was dead."

Even as Mrs. Greene, who'd found us by the water, had shrieked, "What happened? What happened?" I could feel my mind closing in around the words, sealing them up in a way they would never get free. They were still there now, safe from the world. From people who only wanted to know for knowing's sake. Not because any good could come of it.

I'd been pulled here, not just because I wanted to be home with Mrs. Greene and Lacey, but because this was where Mama had been lost. I wanted to turn around and say all those things to Mrs. Greene, to fall into her arms and let her hug it all away for a little while, but there was something about saying the words out loud that would be like writing them down. Saying it out loud would make it After.

Mrs. Greene walked up behind me and stole me away from my thoughts. "Come inside and have some tea."

I held the warm cup between both hands and shadowed Mrs. Greene upstairs to the Fabric Wonderland. She collected fabrics from flea markets and antiques stores and loved to sew quilts in dizzying patterns. She turned on her Elvis Presley gospel music and then sat in her soft wingback chair with a square of purple velvet.

"Can I take some fabric?"

"Help yourself," she said.

I ran my hand over soft velvets and scratchy denim, picking up a cheerful piece of apple-green gingham.

"Your grandma tells me you're still living in her shed."

"I've lived in worse places."

"I know you have. Can you give me a reason?"

Today she wore a yellow sweater. I knew she hung her outfits in the closet color-coordinated, where she'd decide on purple days or red days or blue days. It was always fun to see what she'd turn up in at the breakfast table. I wished everyone were as easy to read.

"It isn't what you think."

"You mean that you're being unreasonable? That you're worrying that poor woman for pure sport? That you're so damn stubborn, you'd rather live in a tin-roofed broken-down shed than give her the satisfaction of sleeping in her house?"

I fussed with the fabrics. "Well, there's that. But on some days, I can hear the river from the house too."

"Oh, Grace." Mrs. Greene looked so sad.

Elvis sang about how he would never walk alone. I closed my eyes and let the sway of his voice talk me into the comfort of that for a while. Then the song ended.

I laid my hand over the fabrics again, wanting them to hum the way the bird parts did with Mama. I wanted to feel certain about something. But nothing happened.

Mrs. Greene asked, "How is it? Being here?"

I didn't know how to answer. I thought about eating her special-occasion French toast with apples and cinnamon, snuggling into the overstuffed chair by the fire, and drinking Earl Grey with lemon and honey, sitting right where I was, with a lifetime of fabric collecting, and the outline image of Mama everywhere. Then I thought about laughing with Lacey as we stuffed our bras. It was all Before.

"It doesn't change anything," I said, rubbing a piece of faded denim.

Mrs. Greene nodded.

"There's something I want to ask you. Promise you won't laugh," I said.

"I'd never laugh at you, Grace."

"I've been finding . . . things. Special things. Do you think it's possible Mama might be trying to tell me something?"

Mrs. Greene took a minute. She looked out the window into the overcast day. "Anything's possible, I suppose. But it's more likely you're trying to tell yourself something. Death is a hard nut to crack."

I didn't know what to think about that.

"Sometimes you see what you want to see because it fits the picture you already have in your head. It's hard to let go of those old pictures and see things as they are."

Which made me think of Grandma. I'd made a decision about her a long time ago: that she was mean and terrible. But living with her, even for this short time, had shown me there was more to her than the worst.

"You will go your whole life, Gracie May, and every single person in it will fail you in one way or another. It's all about the repair. It's all about letting yourself change those pictures."

"Maybe the repair is Grandma's job. Maybe that's why Mama never went back."

"This isn't like a hole in a boat, where you get yourself some wood and some patching and you're good to go. It's a two-person job."

"So maybe I need Grandma to make the first move."

"Hasn't she?"

I had followed Mama for the whole of my life, going from here to there, chasing some idea she had of home, maybe, or running away from what she believed she'd done. Mama was like one of her birds, pieces of lovely all cobbled together with a heart full of sorrow that she'd welded closed. But I didn't have to be that way too.

"Do you know why Mama wanted to leave?"

Mrs. Greene shook her head. "I don't. Especially because we'd just had a conversation about how all the moving had affected you over the years. How she wanted to give you a home. When I tried to ask her why she was leaving, she said she couldn't talk about it, that she might lose her nerve."

Mama had been funny since we saw those sandhill cranes fly over sometime at the end of February. She'd turned irritable. She went for more walks and snapped at me for no good reason. I'd had such high hopes since we got to Mrs. Greene's. Mama had talked about how she understood now that I needed a stable home, and she'd even talked about opening a little shop that only sold cookies and cupcakes, since that was the only kind of cooking she was good at. I even helped her figure out a name. We decided on the Flyaway Bakery.

But then, after those cranes and her mood change, she'd started reading the leaving poem from Robert Frost. She'd thumbtacked the map of California to the wall and had started pacing. For the first time, I stood up to her, told her I wouldn't go. My last words to her were angry ones and I wasn't sure how to live with that, how to fold it in a way that would fit. I wondered if the reason I didn't want to be with Grandma wasn't just because of disloyalty to Mama, but because I was afraid. The only other time I'd tried to claim a place for myself, something horrible had happened.

"I've started over so many times. I don't want to do it again."

"That isn't a good enough reason to stay."

She was right. I loved her. Lacey too. But they weren't my family. I thought how easily a mother and daughter fit together and how anyone else just sort of hung there, like an extra thumb. It suddenly occurred to me that maybe we'd clicked—me and Mama, Lacey and Mrs. Greene—because we walked the same kind of road, one without fathers or husbands. But without Mama there, I was the extra thumb. I started to cry.

Mrs. Greene came over and put her arms around me.

"I always figured everything was Grandma's fault—Mama moving over and over, trying to find a place to fit—but it doesn't feel true anymore."

"What feels true?"

"I don't know. But I do know that Grandma didn't want me."

Mrs. Greene sat me on an ottoman and kneeled down in front of me. "What your grandma didn't want was the situation. There's a big difference."

She smoothed my most stubborn cowlick as I pulled a scrap of pink felt out of a nearby pile and used it to wipe my nose. I had no idea what to do. I felt like one of Mama's birds before she put it together, all pieces and parts in a jumble.

"What feels true?" she asked again.

I closed my eyes. I didn't want to say it. I didn't want to say that I wanted to give Grandma a chance.

21

Goo Bless
You

Lacey moped around as I packed. When Grandma showed up, Lacey disappeared. I looked everywhere, calling, but couldn't find her.

I said good-bye to Mrs. Greene quickly, like ripping off a bandage, and then walked down the front path to where Granny Smith was parked at the curb, Grandma sitting behind the wheel. She wore a sky-blue scarf that made me think of summer and things to come. As I reached the truck, Elvis Presley started blasting from the Fabric Wonderland window.

"*I'LL HAVE A BAHLUUUUE CHRISTMAS WITHOUT YOUUUU.*"

"It's only May!" I called.

The volume turned up.

"*I'LL BE SO BAHLUUUUE JUST THINKING AHAHABOUT YOUUUU.*"

It was hard not to smile as I climbed into the truck, the familiar mix of vinyl, dirt, and gasoline filling my nose. I felt like two whole and entirely different people, one who wanted to stay and one who wanted to go.

Mrs. Greene said, "Send me some poems. Good ones. Can't just be hanging anything on my refrigerator."

"I told you. They aren't for refrigerators."

"Too bad. I don't have much to show off in this world, except for you and Lacey."

Of course Lacey came running out the front door at the last minute, flinging herself at my window. I rolled it down. She'd thrown her hair up into a ponytail this morning, not taking the care with it that she usually did.

"You are smart and funny and you don't need me here reminding you all the time," I said, hugging her through the window. "And you need to stop helping Mrs. Flute with the kindergartners all the time. Stick with Jill and Carrie. They're sweet."

"Okay."

It was the most sad and pathetic *okay* in the history of the world. As Grandma pulled onto the road, I expected Lacey to come hollering after us, the way they do in the movies. She didn't. She and Mrs. Greene stood there on the curb, getting smaller and smaller as we drove away.

Grandma was quiet. We passed fields of swaying emerald grass and trees as we left Sacramento. In one of those fields, set far off the road against a bent-up chain-link fence, were giant red plastic letters. The kind you might see in front of a church declaring JESUS SAVES! Only bigger. They spelled out GOO BLESS YOU. I felt a little spot of warmth for whoever put those letters out. How they weren't about to let a missing *D* get in their way.

"Did you bring Daisy back to your house?" I said as we climbed the hill.

"I did." She adjusted the rearview mirror. "Why did you name her Daisy anyway?"

"Mama said she looked just like a dog turd, and so we had to call her something nice."

This brought the first laugh I'd heard out of Grandma. She squeaked a little when she laughed and I saw she had the same crooked tooth as Mama. I couldn't help but laugh too.

As Grandma drove back through town, I took in the now-familiar redbrick of the old buildings, the huge metal spoon hanging outside Spoons, Margery's red shop awning, and Lafollette's, the place where Mama and Daddy almost made their way into a different life. Instead of feeling a dark and pressing sadness, though, I was starting to feel like maybe I could belong here. It surprised me, that feeling, and I wished it carried over to Grandma. But it didn't.

"Can I stop and talk to Margery?" I said.

Grandma slowed and parked in front of Spoons. "Go ahead. I'll have some coffee and wait."

"You can go on. I'll walk."

"I'd rather wait." She angled the rearview mirror down and checked her face, fidgeting with the hair that had come loose from her bun. She touched a finger to her lips.

I climbed out of the car as a short, plump woman rushed out of Spoons and hurried across the street into Threads.

"Take your time," Grandma said as she shut and locked her door. I saw Sheriff Bergum through the window sitting at the counter in Spoons. So that was why she'd been primping. If she'd been Mama, I would have made little smooching noises, but I didn't think Grandma would take too kindly to that.

I followed the lady into the shop, where she was already explaining to Margery, in accelerating tones, how her bra strap had busted while she was eating a bowl of split pea soup, and the weight of her unhinged ladyhood came flying down and knocked her bowl all over herself. She was teary and full of exclamations, and Margery calmed her down with an oatmeal raisin cookie from the bakery next door and a new 18 Hour bra, whatever that was. I was only wearing mine for nine, tops.

As she was helping Soup Lady, I went around the store, touching things. Silky pajamas, lacy bras, fluffy bathrobes. It was a cozy place to be.

"Your mama used to design my windows," Margery said once the lady had left. Her muumuu was a much softer batch of colors today, and it made me think of Mrs. Greene, how the color of her clothes matched the color of her mood. Maybe Margery was like that too.

"Really?"

Her hair was curly, just past her shoulders, mostly silver with threads of walnut brown. She tossed it behind her shoulders. "Once she and your dad started spending time together, she took over my window. She'd combine her art with different antiques and place the slippers and hosiery just so. Like they were meant to be together. People would gather around when she was designing. One time we even had this fancy photographer come all the way from San Francisco to take pictures of her displays. It was great for business."

"Lou told me she used to steal her spoons."

"Ha!" Margery said. She reached into a low drawer behind her and pulled out a handful of bent spoons. "She sure did. I always thought I might give it a try, put stuff together the way she used to and make something pretty, but I wasn't any good at it."

I fanned the spoons in a circle, bowls facing out so that it looked like a daisy, and thought about Mama's daisy meadow. How I felt certain I'd find the next clue at Spoons.

"Looks like you have the knack," Margery said.

"Not like Mama."

"So what's your knack?"

I didn't want to talk about writing. Instead, I asked my own question. "Did Mama and Grandma ever get along?"

She got up from the zebra-print chair and went over to her bureau of pictures. She pulled one out and handed me a picture of a girl my age and a woman who looked like Mama. I took a sharp breath realizing it was Mama and Grandma.

"They were as different from each other as a monkey is from a pinecone, so that didn't help. Miranda isn't soft around the edges, and people like that can be hard to love. But she loved your mama something fierce."

I set the picture back on the dresser. "Mama said that love was an action, not a word. If Grandma loved Mama so much, she never would have sent her away."

"Sometimes we lose pieces of who we are in times of great sorrow and distress. And then we have to find a way to get them back. Your grandma lost so much of herself when your grandpa died and then when your mama got off that bus." She shook her head.

The truth of that finally hit me—how much Grandma had lost. Her husband and then her daughter. Her granddaughter. I thought about her sitting in her living room by the fire day after day, waiting for her daughter to come home, waiting for a phone call or a letter that never came. For years.

"I think that's why your mama left too. She lost herself. Some people think space is the answer, that somehow in the wide-open they might stumble into answers. Soon enough it's just easier to stay gone."

It should have made me angry, her saying that. But it didn't. Because it was true.

"I've got something for you," Margery finally said. She went through the red velvet curtain behind the counter.

I heard shuffling and then she came out with a small, hard plastic suitcase and set it on the counter.

"Go ahead, open it," she said. She reached one plump hand up and pushed at the fuzzy hairs at her temple.

I flipped the tarnished brass latch and opened the lid. It was an old-fashioned typewriter with a folder of typed pages wedged into the lid. I ran my finger along the pages, flipping them. It was a collection of poems and what looked like short stories.

"It was your father's. His own father had been a writer and your dad wanted to be one too."

I took a step back from the typewriter—stumbled was more like it—as I put a hand up to my mouth. I wanted to jump up and down and spin around. My father had been a writer too.

"He wrote mostly poetry, but kept ideas for a novel."

I smiled. "I have his book of Robert Frost."

"I always wondered where that ended up," Margery said. "That book had belonged to his father, your grand-dad. I think he read it to keep himself close to his parents after they'd died."

"Mama used to read me poems from that book. Every night."

"Did she tell you what those poems were about?"

"She didn't like to look for the meaning stuff. She told me to enjoy the words and not worry about what they meant."

"That's a good thing to do sometimes. But sometimes, you want to know the meaning of a thing. Your dad loved those poems because he thought they were about a boy going out into the world and finding his way, coming home a man. They brought him comfort because they re-minded him of his father, but also because the words gave him confidence, making him feel that he'd find his own way, no matter what."

Words started to trickle into my mind from different Frost poems.

. . . I left you in the morning . . .

. . . Now close the windows and hush all the fields . . .

. . . Give a heart to the hopeless fight . . .

198

"I had hoped your mama took it with her when she left, but I always wondered why she didn't take the typewriter too."

"Probably because a book was easier to take from place to place."

By reading me the poems, Mama said she was filling me up with my father in the only way she could. She was planting words inside my empty places, hoping something would take root and grow. But she never told me he was a poet. That he wanted to write novels. She didn't take his work or his typewriter, things I would have cherished. She didn't tell me stories about him, and I was starting to see that her efforts weren't good enough. She should have set aside some of her own aches and pains so that I wouldn't have so many of my own.

After a while, I asked, "What was his favorite kind of soup?"

"Minestrone."

"What about music? Did he like listening to music?"

"He liked to dance."

I closed my eyes, and when I opened them, he was there in the corner of the room, and so was I, small, my feet on top of his as he danced me around in circles. Where he'd always been this flat image I'd carried around in my pocket, suddenly he was here, right in this room, inside me in a way I hadn't felt before.

He had been someone I would have loved, and I didn't realize what a relief that was until I felt it, through and through. And he would have loved me. I let myself fill up with it, fill up with the knowing that Margery was here and I could ask her anything. Forever.

"Did you help Mama and Daddy get to the Greyhound that night?"

Margery fidgeted with the edge of her sleeve. "Your grandma never forgave me, and I can't say I blame her. Your mama was just seventeen. But I knew your grandparents wanted to send her away and I didn't believe that was right. Scotty had already lost so much. Not many days go by that I don't think about what might have happened if I'd helped them figure things out differently."

Just like the pieces of Mama's cranes, each of us was a piece in her life, and her death. But maybe that's how it was with everything. If you were going to let yourself be connected to people, you had to be willing to take chances.

"Is he buried here somewhere?"

"In the same cemetery as your mama."

I thought about that for a minute. The foreverness of it. It was why I hadn't visited Mama's grave. I just didn't want to see the grass growing over her body, her name engraved in stone.

"Do you think Mama would have wanted me living with Grandma?"

"I don't know, Grace."

Mrs. Greene's didn't feel like the right place anymore, but neither did Grandma's. I thought about my signpost cranes and the clues that were left, still thinking Mama was trying to help. To show me where I belonged.

"Can I take these?" I gestured to the spoons.

"Make something pretty," she said, and came around the counter to give me a hug. She was only an inch or so taller than I was and I let my head rest on her shoulder. She smelled like the bakery next door.

I pulled away.

"Home is in your hands, Grace." She gestured around her store and then gave me a bag for the spoons. "Sometimes you have to make a place for yourself."

I gave her another hug, tight around her waist, and took off for Spoons and whatever clue Mama had waiting.

22

Tangled

I walked into the Spoons Souperie, the cowbell ringing above my head, and when lots of people turned from their soup-slurping to look at me, I felt like a gunslinger coming to town. If Mama had been wiping one of the tables, or busy at the condiment station, I would have twitched my hand above my hip and grabbed something like a banana or a coat hanger and drawn it. She would have clutched her chest and spun around, and we would have laughed to pieces.

Instead, Grandma smiled and took her giant black purse off the seat next to her, Sheriff Bergum winked and went back to his berry pie, and Archer scurried away from the table he'd been busing, disappearing into the kitchen, where there was a loud and long clattering, as if he'd launched himself into a mountain of silverware.

I sat down on the red stool next to Grandma and laid out my spoons on the counter. "For Mama's crane," I said.

Grandma smiled again. "When it's done, we'll hang it wherever you like."

I nodded, wondering if she'd let me hang it in my shed.

Lou hurried over. "Please tell me you aren't going to be stealing my spoons too!" She and Grandma laughed.

"I don't think Miss Grace here wants to overfamiliarize herself with my jail cell," Sheriff Bergum said, laughing along.

Even I smiled at that. But I came here for a reason. "Did Mama leave anything here?"

"What do you mean, sweetie?" Lou said as she wiped her crepe-paper hands on a white towel.

"I don't know. Did you ever find anything in the lost and found that might have belonged to her, or . . ." I was grasping. I had no idea what I was looking for. "Did she make anything for your restaurant? A piece of junk art, maybe? Did she paint or draw something?"

The elusive Mel came out from the kitchen with his famous ladle and pointed toward the room where the comfy chairs were. He had a very large, round, and red nose. There wasn't much hair on top of his head, just a thin covering, like he'd spread what little was left with a butter knife.

"There is one thing, I guess," Lou said, following Mel's ladle. "But your mama didn't take the photograph."

I jumped up from the stool. "Where?"

Lou slung her towel over one shoulder as she came from behind the counter. Her shoes squeaked as she walked across the floor.

I followed her into the cozy room, and she pointed to a fancy-looking black-and-white photograph of Mama's fountain in Bear River Park. Hanging beside it were three framed sketches of different bird and wing designs, signed in Mama's curly handwriting.

"Your mama was so talented," Lou said, beaming at the photo and sketches.

Mama never made her clues easy. I always had to use imagination and craftiness to figure out where to go next. The good thing about her treasure hunts from Before, though, was that everyone was in on it, so when I'd get stuck, someone was around to give me a nudge.

This time, I had to rely on my gut, this flimsy little thing that didn't seem to know up from down anymore. I almost wanted to tell Lou or Margery or Grandma. But how do you tell someone that you believed your mama, who had passed along, was still near, like that wavy heat coming off the asphalt on a hot summer day? My own best friend didn't even believe me.

Nope, I was alone in all this.

Lou dusted the glass of the photograph with her white

towel. "We were so glad to have a place for Billy's tree house. He helped Mel build it in our yard when he was ten years old and we thought to keep it for the grandkids when they came. When he died, it was too hard to look at it right outside the windows. But it would have been harder to take it down." She smiled a sad smile. "When your grandma designed the park, with all those different projects in mind, it was the perfect answer for us. So Mel took down the tree house, one plank at a time, and rebuilt it. Now we can visit when we need to. Mel has been known to nap up there on a warm summer day, even went as far as to build a wooden sign that lets people know when it's occupied."

She pointed to the photograph of Mama's fountain. "Your grandma tends to that fountain and her park like they were actual blood and bone family."

"So I've heard," I said.

She looked at me, took the curve of my cheek in her hand. "We've been waiting for you."

I was so caught off guard by what she said that all I could do was thank her and ask for a minute to myself, where I slumped down in a soft leather chair. It never occurred to me that other people besides Grandma had wondered about me and Mama, hoping we'd come back.

After a little while, Archer came around the corner

with a glass of something and sat in the chair next to me. "Here, I made you my favorite," he said. "It's called an Arnold Palmer. Half lemonade, half iced tea."

"No way," I said. "That's my favorite too."

"Really? I took you for the Shirley Temple type."

"Ha."

We sat there for a second, looking at everything but each other.

"How do you work here, anyway? You're not old enough to have a job."

"Lou is my grandfather's sister." He shrugged. "They like having me around."

I noticed he had one dark freckle on his earlobe and one close to it on his jaw. I had the urge to take a pen and draw a line from one to the other.

"I was worried you might not come back," he said.

I liked the way he could be flustered one minute and direct the next. It made me see I wasn't by myself with my own tangled feelings.

The sun was setting in a burst of orange with rain-cloud slivers. It took up the whole sky.

"Are there lights in the park?" I said.

If he thought that was a strange question, he didn't look it. "Nope."

So I'd have to wait until tomorrow to go to the fountain.

"Archer Lee Hamilton!" Lou shrieked from the restaurant side.

"Gotta go," Archer said, and zoomed around the corner.

I stood up and looked again at the photograph of Mama's fountain, the sketches beside it, thinking about Grandma's hard work. How she probably would have traded it all, the park, the fountain, maybe even her own garden, to have us back. I didn't know for sure if that was true. But it felt true. "I'm counting on you to show me the way," I whispered. I touched my lips and then touched the cold glass of the photograph, missing Mama so much, my bones ached.

23

A Home
of My Own

My feelings scooted from one side of things to the other and then back again. Over and over until finally, they crashed so hard to one side, I felt sure they might just knock me flat. Grandma wasn't this horrible person I'd made her out to be. But that didn't mean I could trust her. She couldn't erase what she'd done with all the good deeds in the world because, in the end, what if I made a bad decision? Would she put me on a bus to Texas? I didn't want to go to Texas. It's hot, and there are cows everywhere.

Thinking can steal the magic right out of a thing, Mama's voice echoed in my head.

So I tried really hard not to think as Grandma drove me to school on Tuesday. Mama had been gone a month and it still felt like I could turn around and she'd be there, arms wide, telling me it had all been a mistake.

Grandma walked me in to excuse my absence and then went into Mr. Flinch's office and closed the door, leaving me to wait for Mrs. Turner to give me a pass. Grandma would have to make it fast, though, since first period was about to start, and Mr. Flinch had to get to class.

Mrs. Turner's nails were long and white-tipped and they clicked extra loud on the computer keys. She wore her dyed brown hair in a short bob, frozen in place with hairspray so that it looked like a helmet. I was mesmerized by how she whisked herself from one end of the desk to the other, dug through drawers and printed things, answered the phone and leaned down to pick up a dropped pencil, all without that hair moving one square inch.

She slid a small pink absence form onto the counter, phone between her shoulder and ear, and as she filled it out, I noticed an origami crane sitting next to the pencil holder. Just sitting there plain as day. This one was bright pink and the paper was crumpled as though someone had fished it out of the trash before folding it. It seemed Mr. Flinch's cranes had a way of getting around.

I waited until she hung up. "Where did you get that?"

"It showed up a couple of days ago, like so many things do. You would not believe what has come into this office. Retainers, a fake tarantula, a tiny red box of baby teeth." She slapped her hand on the counter. "One morning, there was a bag of dirt sitting right here on my counter. Dirt, I tell you."

I touched the crane. It was another signpost. Mama was telling me I was on the right track even though I had no idea what I might be looking for at the fountain. Instead of feeling excited, though, it made me tired.

"You look like you could use some toast," Mrs. Turner said. She took a bag of bread from a deep drawer and set a piece into a toaster sitting right there between her computer and printer. "Toast can fix most things."

As Mrs. Turner answered another phone call, I watched through the glass of Mr. Flinch's door and tried to read lips as best I could. *Banana charger in the pig sink wind.* That was the best I came up with. I smiled at my own weird thoughts.

The toast popped and Mrs. Turner slathered on something chocolaty. Then she cut a banana in half lengthwise, careful with her long nails, and wrapped the bread around it like a burrito. She pointed to the little crane.

"I bet this is from Mr. Flinch's class project. But isn't it fun to think maybe it's from a secret admirer? Or that it floated in here, all by itself, to remind me to have a good day? So many possibilities."

She stuck her pencil behind her ear and stared off into the distance, looking dreamy.

"I like your possibilities," I said, and took a bite. "Yum."

"I don't know much, but I do know that if people ate more toast, there might just be world peace." She licked her fingers. "World peace, I tell you."

. . .

As I opened my locker, I saw Max in the hall, head down, feet dragging.

"What's up, Max? Did you forget your lunch again?"

He walked toward me and swung his suitcase around so he could lean his elbow on the handle. "No. I'm thinking too much about kittens."

"Kittens?"

"Because I won't choose anything but an entombment party for my birthday, Mom and Jo are threatening to make it a kitten party. Do you know what the guys will do to me if there are kittens at my party?"

He seemed so serious for someone who was eight years old. I liked that about him. "I'm sorry, Max," I offered.

"It's not your fault."

He walked me to class. When we stopped at the door, I looked at him, really saw him. The way he didn't go anywhere without his red suitcase or bandages on his hands. How he was completely obsessed with mummies and entombment and no one was listening. He seemed so sad and desperate and it reminded me of me.

"Maybe I could talk to Jo?"

"Really?" Max looked hopeful.

"Sure. But I'm not promising anything. Don't give up," I said, just as much for myself as for Max.

He gave me a tight squeeze around my waist. The

bandages on his hands were getting dirty around the edges.

"Never," he said.

Jo and Beth still weren't speaking, and their pesky anger went with us from class to class. Beth and Ginger had taken to wearing matching T-shirts that said things like FORGIVENESS IS THE ANSWER or HOME IS WHERE THE SPLEEN IS. It seemed like a dig at Jo, them not including her in their T-shirt plans, and Jo was sulky all morning, but I didn't get a chance to talk to her until art.

"Your grandma told me you got in a fight when I came by on Saturday," Jo said as I sat down at our table. She was writing notes in her documentary binder. "Then she came over on Sunday for coffee and said you were at your old house for a couple of days."

"I'm sorry I didn't call or anything."

She fidgeted in her seat and then looked over her shoulder to make sure no one was listening. Beth and Ginger's table was fairly close. She whispered, "I know Sheriff Bergum put you in a jail cell."

I expected to be angry. It was my business. Not hers or anyone else's. But I wasn't. I just didn't want to talk about it.

"I'll never tell," she went on. "I only heard bits and pieces anyway because they sent me out of the room and kept their voices low. I put a glass to the wall, but I guess that only works in movies."

Beth and Ginger were practically leaning sideways, they were listening so hard.

I whispered as quietly as I could, "Does anyone else know?"

"I don't think so. But Ginger's mom is the worst gossip in town." She glared over my shoulder at Ginger but didn't raise her voice. "I honestly think she's a witch or something because she always knows things she shouldn't."

Just then, Beth got up from her table and went over to her box frame on the wall. She took out the PEACE stone and set her label maker inside.

As Beth came back toward us, Jo said, "How will you ever survive without it?"

Instead of answering, Beth set the PEACE stone in front of Jo. Before Jo had a chance to react, Beth went back to her own stool and sat down.

"For how can friends be torn asunder while peace is at their beck and call?" Ginger said, one arm reaching toward the ceiling as though asking the question of God himself.

Archer and Stubbie clapped. Ginger stood up and took a bow, her peanut hair falling in a cascade to the floor. She swept it back in a flourish.

Jo flicked Beth's PEACE rock across the table, where it tumbled to a stop in front of me.

"I think she's trying to apologize," I whispered.

"Yeah. But it won't change anything," Jo said, looking even gloomier than before.

"Can I ask you a favor?" I said to Jo, whispering again, thinking I could distract her from her misery.

"Sure."

"Do you think I could look over your research on the Bear River Park and my mom's fountain?"

She lit up. "I can bring it by today after school."

"How about we meet at the fountain?" I said.

"How about we take the horses out? I've been wanting to take you riding. There are some horse trails in the park."

Just then, a spitball landed right between us. Jo and I both looked over at Stubbie and Archer's table. Stubbie was busy pretending to be innocent while Archer took his artist's mannequin—one of those weird little wooden doll things that you could bend into different positions—and waved its hand at us. I smiled and he turned pink.

"Okay, class, it's the moment we've all been waiting for. The other half of the self-portrait."

Mrs. Snickels plopped a brown grocery bag filled with goodies on our table, then she set down a couple of empty paper lunch sacks beside it. Once she was finished distributing bags at each table, she went to her desk and clipped her newly fashioned portrait to the whiteboard. Her fingers were covered with smears of blue and green paint.

"It's called a split-faced self-portrait. For obvious reasons, I hope," Mrs. Snickels said.

I recognized her portrait from my first day of school. Only now, the other half was filled with collage. She'd painted a tree with a swing, drawn in different shapes and colors, and glued down words from magazines and newspapers, scattering them around like confetti. It made me think about how my own brain must look, with words floating around all the time. How my father's and grandfather's brains must have looked the same way. It made me smile to think of it.

"These will be due next week, so over the next couple of days, I want you to consider what you might put on the abstract side. Really consider it. And then start to compile. Phrases that your dad always says. A snatch of fabric. Hopes for the future. When you're done compiling, compose your abstract, and . . . ?"

"Don't glue it down!" everyone said.

"Why not?"

"Because we aren't perfect!"

"Right. So don't glue down the mistakes. Give yourself room to change your mind. To reevaluate. Inside the bag you'll find items that might give you inspiration. But

I want you to work on these at home, and don't show anyone. That's what the smaller bags are for. Load them up with whatever you like. I have a contest in mind for the finished product."

Jo blurted, "Is this the Observation of the Month?"

"Yes!"

The class broke out in a case of murmurs, and Jo told me that every month, Mrs. Snickels put together some kind of contest to see if they'd been paying attention to the world. There were prizes.

When the bell rang, she came by our table. "Grace. Before you go, can I have a word? I'll give you a pass."

As the kids filed out, Mrs. Snickels sat on Jo's stool and I looked at her across the pockmarked and paint-stained table, her black hair pulled up into a short, messy ponytail. She had a file folder and a brown paper package.

"So how are you doing on the year-end project? Any ideas?"

"I'm a little lost, but I'm sure I'll think of something."

She nodded and pushed the package toward me.

"It's a sketchpad. I noticed you didn't have one. For your sketching. And your poetry."

I shook my head. There was no way she could know about my words. I'd never showed anyone but Mama, Mrs. Greene, and Lacey. Plus they'd only been living in my head for the last few weeks.

"Th-thank you," I finally stuttered. "How did you know?"

She didn't answer. Instead, she took a paper-sized piece of poster board out of the file and set it in front of me, my bumpy ten-year-old's signature scrawled on the bottom left corner. My breath caught. The last time I'd seen the collage was in fifth grade for an art contest, two moves before Mrs. Greene. There was a blue ribbon taped to the back. First place.

"How did you get this?"

"It was tucked into a big envelope with some other stuff when you transferred here, so it must have gotten overlooked before now."

I picked it up, my fourth-grade friend Pippy flashing to mind. How she'd collect everyone's plastic bags at lunch and then cut them up with these tiny blunt-ended scissors she brought each day. Said she was afraid some bird would find their way into the plastic and not find their way out again. She was working for a good cause, so I joined her with my own pair of scissors. We'd see who could make the most interesting shape out of the cut-up plastic. One day she made a profile of Abraham Lincoln and ended up giving it to the assistant principal because everyone knew about Mr. Hobbs and how he liked to reenact the Civil War. He hung it in his office, where it was probably still hanging today.

When Mama and I moved on from Stockton to Lodi, I sat alone at lunch, again, saving my plastic bags, missing Pippy. After I had a pile, I cut them into strips, braided them into ropes and hot-glued them into the shape of a fanciful house. Then I glued all manner of things to the house: sequins, buttons, Easter basket grass, bottle caps, peacock feathers sprouting from the roof. The finishing touch was a poem I'd written inside the front door.

I am like the little avocado seed
Mama likes to settle
into a shallow bowl of water
on the windowsill
in the sunlight.
The roots grow and grow,
down and around
and up along the underside of the pit,
safe from the world.

You'd think after moving fourteen times, I'd have it down by then. But once in a while, my roots would sneak into the ground without my noticing. It wasn't until we left that I'd feel the ripping sadness as they pulled free.

Mrs. Snickels pointed to the poem on the collage. "There you are. Tucked right inside this poem."

I didn't even realize until right then that I'd been lost.

Not just since Mama died, but before then too. If I was honest, I left a little piece of myself behind in every place we'd ever lived, felt so much pressure that I had to worry about things when Mama didn't. I should have said something a long time before I did instead of keeping myself wrapped up in my little glass bowl. Maybe things would have turned out different if I had.

"It must have been hard going to all those different schools."

I picked at my thumbnail. "It was."

"Listen, I'd like to set the collage in your box. This way, I don't have to look at an empty frame anymore. It's murder on my need for orderliness."

I took in her cluttered desk and matching shelves behind it. There was a smudge of red paint on her cheekbone and all over her blue striped button-down shirt. She had a tiny white feather in her hair.

"I'd like to keep it," I said.

"When you're good and ready, then."

I stared at all the box frames on the wall. My eyes went right to Archer's. He had a sketch of Ladle Boy doing yoga. Stubbie's held a magazine called *Old Fishing Lures and Tackle*. Ginger had taken out her *Wicked* Playbill and put in a flyer for Shakespeare in the Park at Bear River Park. Jo's still had the tiny director's chair.

I looked at my box frame with my name underneath. I

hadn't given much thought to the emptiness of it until just now. But when I searched my mind for what might belong there, I came up blank.

Mrs. Snickels caught me looking at my frame. She walked over to her desk and scrounged around, coming up with a pinecone. She handed it to me.

"Sometimes we just need to fill the hollow spaces with what's handy until we're ready for what's true."

I took the pinecone and set it in the frame, feeling a small rush of warmth. What was empty just seconds ago wasn't empty anymore, and I wished everything could be that easy.

24

The Other Side

At lunch I called Grandma from Mr. Flinch's office to make sure it was okay to go to the Brannigans for horseback riding after school, and Jo called her mom. I could hear Mrs. Brannigan's happy exclamations through the phone even though Jo was standing a good two feet away. Jo smiled at me and gave a thumbs-up. It was nice to be wanted.

After school the Brannigan and Son truck pulled up with Mrs. Brannigan waving like a crazy person. Her hair was the color of eggshells, almost white it was so blond, and it blew in the breeze of her open window. I hadn't noticed before how young she looked, and so much like Jo, down to the turned-up nose and small ears except rounder.

"I'm so glad you're coming over today!" Mrs. Brannigan gushed. "Mr. Brannigan is so glad too!"

"Thanks for having me," I said.

I climbed into the back of the cab with Max. He looked at me meaningfully, as though we shared a secret. Which,

I supposed, we did. I understood his strange need for an entombment party in a way his family didn't, and somehow, that felt like a secret. Weird as it was.

After we pulled away from the curb, Mrs. Brannigan looked at Max through the rearview mirror and asked a series of questions. How was your day? How did you do on your report? Did you make up with Spencer? When he didn't answer, her forehead crinkled with frustration. Max sat with his bandaged arms tightly wrapped around his suitcase and stared out the window.

"Still ignoring me, huh?" Mrs. Brannigan said.

Silence.

"Well, I guess I'll have to keep talking until you talk back." Then she went on about how some people can just make their own yellow food and wash their own yellow sheets.

Jo said, "Mom! Please. Can't you wait until after Grace leaves to be . . . crazy?"

"I have a good mind not to let you go fishing today," Mrs. Brannigan said to Max, ignoring Jo altogether.

Max perked right up. "You wouldn't!"

"I would. The least you can do is give one-word answers. Yes. No. Fine. I'll even throw some in a hat and you can pick one out."

Jo turned around in her seat. "Stubbie takes Max

fishing every other week if the weather's good." Then she said to her mom, "You can't take fishing away!"

"Stubbie Wilkins?" I said.

"The one and only."

Jo, Max, and Mrs. Brannigan continued to bicker. I took a deep breath and let everything wash over me. The way you can ask for help and people will actually give it. The surprising feeling of belonging as I sat in the middle of a squabbling family when I'd just left Mrs. Greene's feeling the opposite. The idea of riding a horse for the very first time.

Mrs. Brannigan turned into her driveway just as Stubbie got out of an old blue Ford Bronco. Before I could get out of the car, Max pressed something into my hand. A mummy in a tiny sarcophagus. "Thanks for listening to me before," he said and then climbed out.

"Hello, Mrs. Brannigan," Stubbie said as he walked up to us.

"Hello, Warren. Be back in an hour or so, would you? No later than an hour and a half. Max has some extra reading to do tonight."

"Mom!" Max said, pleading.

All she had to do was put both hands on her hips and glare. Without a word, Max turned around and headed toward the back of the house, head hanging, kicking at rocks.

Stubbie gave Jo a quick sideways glance. "Hi, Jo. Grace."

"Hey, Stubbie," Jo said.

He ran both hands through his spikey red hair and then shoved them in his back pockets. "Well, um . . . it's a good day for fishing."

"It sure is. Shouldn't you go after my brother? He's getting away."

"Right!" He said, and hurried off after Max, turning to wave just before disappearing behind the house.

I looked at Jo and smiled. "He totally likes you."

"No. He's just a goofball."

"Well, yeah. But he totally likes you."

Jo puffed up a little. "Do you think so?"

"I think so."

"Ugh. All I see when I look at him is his preschool self putting a worm down my pants."

"Admit it. He makes you laugh."

"I'll never admit anything."

Mrs. Brannigan had already gone inside and as we came through the door, she was standing in front of a floor-to-ceiling bookshelf lined with containers of every shape and size. There were beautiful pottery jars and a small metal box with a dragonfly lid. There were Kerr jam jars, too, like the one that held my origami cranes, only these were filled with slips of paper.

She reached into one of the Kerrs and pulled one out. After reading it, she held it close to her heart and then shoved it into the pocket of her orange sweater.

"Come on, girls, let me pack you some snacks."

"Already done," Mr. Brannigan said as he came around the corner with a portable cooler.

Mr. Brannigan was tall and lanky where Mrs. Brannigan was small and round so that together they looked like a lowercase *b* or *d* depending which side of him she was standing on. He wore a brown cowboy hat and work boots and had a chin full of brownish-red stubble, which he rubbed with long fingers.

"So, you ready to ride a horse today, Grace?" he said.

"I am," I said, and gulped, because I wasn't really ready at all. Horses were tall and liked to trot and I was afraid of tumbling off.

He handed Jo the cooler and then put his hand on top of her head as though it were a basketball. "I'll meet you in the barn," he said and winked at me. Just that little wink made me feel a whole lot better.

As he walked out the sliding glass door, Jo scooted over to Mrs. Brannigan and pointed toward her sweater pocket. "What did it say?"

"'Have a sit in the shade,'" she said.

Jo nodded. After gathering her Bear River park re-search and loading it into her backpack with her camera, she took my arm and steered me outside. As we marched across the grassy field toward the barn, I kept staring at her backpack, thinking the answer to the next clue might just be that close.

The Brannigans had loads of land, flossy green hills, trees scattered in groups of pines and cedars, a thick rocky stream feeding into a deep swimming pond with a dock and raft, a fenced-off barn at the back. A family of geese sat on the bank of the pond. I couldn't see any houses other than Grandma's off to the right, just a hint of blue through the lacework of trees.

"Just when you thought we couldn't be more loony tunes, all those jars on the bookshelf? Those are my mom's Answer Jars. When she figures something out, she writes it down and then sticks it in a jar. When something comes up and we don't know what to do, we consult the jars." She wrapped her scarf tight around her neck. "I know it sounds weird, but it works. Well, mostly . . ."

"Doesn't sound weird to me."

The horses grazed in the pasture, each as different as the pines were from the oaks or the cedars. Beauty came to me from where she stood and nudged my hand.

"When is her baby due?"

"Should be within the week."

Jo introduced the rest. Raven was black as pitch and belonged to her father, who loved Edgar Allan Poe and any kind of story that might raise your hairs in the dark of night. Beauty was her mother's. White with bluish-gray splotches, she liked to flick her mane about and prance as though preparing for a beauty contest. When she wasn't pregnant, that is.

Pumpkin and Shade were in the barn with Mr. Brannigan.

"When I was younger, I'd sit under that tree over there and read, and Shade would come and stand right over me, blocking the sun. He was named Fudge, but I got to calling him Shade, and he liked it better," Jo said.

"They're beautiful."

"Have you ever ridden?"

"Nope."

"Max named Pumpkin because he is the color of a pumpkin. So original! The horse is sweet, though."

Mr. Brannigan helped me saddle Pumpkin while Jo saddled Shade. He named everything as we went. First there was a saddle pad, then a fancy red-and-white-checked blanket. Next he helped me lift the saddle, which weighed about a thousand pounds, onto the horse. He showed me how to tighten the front and back cinches, warning me to always double-check them before climbing into the stirrups.

His face was lined and tan, like he lived outdoors, and he smelled like fresh-cut wood. He put his hands on either side of my waist and helped me into the saddle whether I was ready or not.

"How does it feel up there?" he said, and patted Pumpkin on his haunches.

"Good," I said, and I wasn't lying.

"Just sit tall and straight, don't lean forward or backward. And no flapping elbows! That is terrible form and we can't have you riding around looking like a chicken."

I smiled at that and felt myself ease into the saddle even more.

"Don't worry," Jo said from the back of her horse. "Horses have been known to read your mind after a while, if you let them. So don't just yank the reins; lead the horse with your whole self and you'll get where you're going. At least that's what Dad always says."

Mr. Brannigan took Pumpkin's reins and led us outside. Once we were at the trail that ran parallel to Ridge Road, he said, "Both reins in one hand. Relax like Jo said and you'll be fine."

Once we got going, I turned around and gave Mr. Brannigan a small wave. He saluted and went back into the barn.

We led them, Shade and Pumpkin, down the hard-packed trail. The saddle was stiff but comfortable.

Jo took it slow and steady. When the trail widened, we walked the horses side by side for a long time. The sun was warm when it slid out from behind the clouds. I closed my eyes and felt like I'd grown bigger somehow, like I had more room inside.

"Did you want to get together this weekend and search for your meadow?" Jo said.

"I sort of found it already."

"You did?" Jo seemed happy. "Where was it?"

"Walking distance from Grandma's."

"Isn't that how it is with most things? You screech for your mom to help you find your shoes and they end up being right under your nose." Jo suddenly looked stricken. "I'm sorry, I didn't mean to talk about . . ."

"It would be weirder if you never talked about your mom."

There was a crosswalk in the middle of Main Street, so we used it and walked up the side of the road toward the park.

I took Max's mummy out of my pocket and showed it to Jo. "Max is upset about his kitten party."

"So now he's harassing you too?" She sighed heavily.

"No. He was just sad. Why won't you let him have his party? Is it against your religion or something?"

"It's unhealthy, that's all."

She leaned toward me as though she might say something, but then she didn't.

About five minutes later, we came to a long curve in the trail, and then the park. It was just as I'd remembered it, all piney green and secret pathways.

"There's a trail along the outside edge, and a place we can tie the horses," Jo said.

I followed her under a canopy of trimmed tree branches that felt like passing into a fairy forest with twinkling hummingbird feeders, birdhouses, and other kinds of interesting objects hanging from the trees: a toilet seat cover spray-painted red, an old rusty mailbox with the red flag raised, and a surfboard, which made me think of my father. I decided right then and there I would learn to surf.

The dirt path led to a watering trough for the horses and an old-fashioned hitching post. Jo went to her pack for carrots and the cooler. We fed the carrots to the horses and then Jo led me through the trees to Mama's fountain. It gave me the same feeling of wonder to see it again.

There were so many details, layers of curved and flat pieces of metal so that if you tilted your head, they might look like waves. The steel waves of an overcast day. But those bits of metal also looked like wings, all different kinds, from tiny hummingbird wings to the giant wings of an eagle. I supposed you could see what you wanted to see, depending on what you were looking for.

Jo spread the blanket in a patch of sunlight between

two trees, the sun lighting up the reddish tint of her brown hair. As soon as we sat, though, the clouds moved the sunlight out of reach. She took a big yellow envelope out of her backpack and handed it to me.

There was a smoochy couple sitting on the edge of the fountain and a small short-haired dog running around in circles chasing its tail. A jogger went by, running for her life, it seemed, and wearing a fluorescent pink shirt most likely visible from heaven. A woman sat in a fold-out beach chair and read a book. She wore a baseball hat and dark sunglasses.

The folder had lots of newspaper clippings from when the park was being suggested to the city council, the different park ideas that were tossed around, and the final plan. There were blueprints and schematics and some quotes Jo had written down from her interviews.

It just seemed so strange. How Grandma could make this place where everyone wanted to be, but she couldn't do that in her own house, with her own daughter and granddaughter.

As I read, Jo put on her beret and took her camera over to the people at the fountain, asking if she could interview them about the park. About ten minutes later, she moved on to some dog walkers while I read through everything she had in the folder. None of it helped me understand

how this fountain was a clue, though, what I might find
here. I got up to read the plaque again with the clip of
Robert Frost's poem.

Where the bird was before it flew,
Where the flower was before it grew,
Where bird and flower were one and the same.

The first time Jo brought me to the park, I'd wanted
those words to mean leaving. But now I wasn't sure what
I wanted. I didn't know what else to look for. Where to go
from here.

"It seems like you're trying to figure something out,"
Jo said. She took off her beret and put the camera away.
"In case I haven't told you, I am a master sleuth. I've read
every single Sherlock Holmes and Agatha Christie novel
in my parents' house. Of which there are many."

"I'll keep that in mind."

She sat down on the blanket and patted the place next
to her. "Let me see that mummy."

I reached in my pocket and handed it to her, then sat
down and crisscrossed my legs.

"I should have told you before," Jo said. She set the
mummy down and laid out our food in a perfect square.
Tiny triangles of peanut butter and jelly sandwiches, a
basket of strawberries, potato chips, and two thick wedges

of chocolate cake. "Max has been sick. He's got something called acute lymphoblastic leukemia, a form of cancer. He's been in remission a little less than a year now."

I didn't know what to say at first. "Remission is good, right?"

"Remission isn't cured," she said, and then took a mouthful of chocolate cake. "Sorry if that was weird to tell you."

But it wasn't weird.

She explained what it had been like, having Max so sick, losing his hair and having to take so many different pills. How she couldn't ever sleep very well thinking he wasn't safe in the night.

"The Other Side is closer to us at night, I think. Waiting there, just ready to pounce," she said.

I nodded some more because I knew a thing or two about the Other Side and how it pounced in the middle of the night. It was nice to be sitting across from someone else in the world who understood, even though that understanding came from something sad. "Is that why you have short hair?" I said.

"I cut it off when Max lost his hair. So did my mom and dad," she laughed. "We looked ridiculous!"

Eventually the sun found its way back to our blanket and warmed my hair and shoulders, and something inside me sprang loose. I could almost hear the metallic *plooong* as some invisible wire, some important cable holding certain things down, snapped free.

"My mother died in the river," I said. "It was an accident."

Jo touched my hand. "I know. I'm real sorry, Grace. I wish I could have known her."

I tried to say more, but my throat closed over the rest of the words and wouldn't let them free.

"Can I ask you something?" Jo said after a while.

"Okay."

"Why are you living in the shed out by the road?"

I shrugged. "I don't know. I'm mad, I guess. About lots of things. And I can hear the river in the house sometimes."

"Well, I can't fix the mad. But I've got an extra pair of great earplugs. I used to wear them when I'd sleep with Max in the hospital."

I almost laughed at how easy that was. I couldn't move the river or Grandma's house. But I could block the sounds if it got to be too much.

I looked around the park and breathed deeply, taking in early spring—the honey scent of flowers, the sweet-sour smell of cut grass, the wildness of growing things and how it all reminded me of little kids after they'd been cooped up too long.

"Can I ask *you* something?" I said.

"I guess it wouldn't be fair if I said no."

"It's pretty and all. But why did you pick this place for your documentary?"

She smiled. "Before he got sick, Max and I would hide in the trees of the park and make up this whole world with our own rules, like the ability to make time stand still and laws against needles and green Jell-O. When he got sick, he just wanted to be in the trees. He said the cancer couldn't get worse if he was here."

She looked up toward the sun and closed her eyes for a minute. "I've always known there were special areas in the park, like Billy's tree house or your mama's fountain. But mostly it was just this place where I'd come to play with my brother and listen to music on summer nights. Once he got sick, though, it turned into something else. I would come by myself and talk to the trees when no one was looking. It felt like they were, I don't know, listening. All I know was that I'd come into the park feeling like I'd never be happy again, and leave feeling there was a chance.

"You probably think I'm crazy," she said.

"I've known crazier," I said, and we both laughed.

I did understand. I felt that way myself at Mama's fountain. But maybe it was more than just the fountain. It was the whole place. This park was almost like a living version of Mama's birds, collecting feelings so people might breathe a little easier. I hoped Mama was in a place where she could breathe easy too.

I gave the fountain the once-over, scanning it from top to bottom, but still didn't know what I was looking for. As much as I liked Jo, and even though she'd just told me something really personal, I couldn't get myself to tell her about Mama and the signs. My own best friend didn't believe me. It was one thing to believe in the Other Side, it was something else entirely to say you had proof.

"I'm furious with him, you know?" Jo said. "For fighting with his friends and wanting an entombment party instead of a normal laser tag party, and with my mother for making everything yellow and still not being back to her normal self. Then I get mad at myself for being mad at them."

I understood that too. How angry I was at Grandma and Mama. At myself.

We packed up the food and walked back toward the horses, who were calm and still, maybe even snoozing in the sunshine.

"Do you get tired of thinking about everything all the time, how things might turn out or not turn out?" I said.

"Really, really tired," Jo said. "Come on, you ready to let these horses run?"

I wasn't, but I followed her lead and found myself as close to real flying as I'd ever been.

25

Building
a Memory

The sun went down and Mrs. Brannigan busied herself filling the kitchen with garlic and onion smells. As Jo edited the footage on her laptop at the kitchen table, I snuck into the dim living room, where the Answer Jars sat on the shelves. I closed my eyes and asked, once and for all, if Mama really was trying to tell me something. Something important. When I was sure my question had floated around long enough, I reached into a green-tinted Kerr jar and pulled out a pink slip of paper. I held it close to my chest, took a deep breath, and read my message. *Three eggs,* it said.

Figuring the Great Beyond must not have heard me correctly, I reached in and took another slip of paper. This one said, *Beach sand.*

There was beach sand in my duffel. One of the few things I'd saved and brought with me from place to place. I thought about that long-ago day on the beach with Mama and wondered what it might have to do with anything.

"What are you doing?" Max stood on the steps, studying me.

"I'm not sure." I put the notes back in the jar and sat down on the bottom step. "So, Jo told me why they don't want you to have your entombment party. Why didn't you tell me?"

"I wanted you to think I was normal."

I laughed. Then he laughed too.

"Jo and your parents are pretty set against it."

"Exactly." Max sat down next to me and picked at the carpet.

The phone rang in the distance and then Mrs. Brannigan called, "Grace, your grandma asked you to come over now. Jo can walk you."

"So what now?" I asked Max.

He raised and then dropped his knobby shoulders.

Exactly.

I thought about what Mrs. Greene had said about Grandma's trying, and what Jo had told me about her fretting over the decoration of Mama's room. I thought about Grandma's own confession to snooping through my things, trying to get a sense of who I was, maybe. What might be important to me.

Then I realized I wasn't sure myself sometimes.

But one thing I did know. I was cold out here in the shed. And now I had earplugs.

I took down my dish towel curtains and folded the rag rug. I tucked Mama's clothes, sheets, two frying pans, and the kitchen utensils into a box and carried it out to Daisy's trunk. Which was a ways off now that Grandma insisted Daisy be parked next to the front porch. She had parked Granny Smith behind her for good measure.

I packed the other box with Mama's quilt, our two photo albums, all my treasure-hunt clues, and my duffel. It made me think about moving to a new place, how Mama only ever let me tape stuff to the walls—magazine cutouts, artwork and stuff. We'd buy this special two-sided tape that wouldn't leave so much as a smidge on the paint. That's how it had always been with Mama. Taping things up in a way that was easy to take down.

The last thing I did was open my backpack and take out the tube that held my self-portrait. I laid it on the flower-garden sofa. Half a girl.

Try as I might to hold them off, pictures came: the silent whirling lights of the ambulance, Mama's matted hair, a policeman standing frozen on the bank of the river with helpless hands stuffed in his pockets.

I tried to get my mind to settle on good pictures of Mama instead, a purple scarf in her hair, digging in some small snatch of dirt to plant tomatoes, the smile on her face each morning when she saw me for the first time, the faraway look she had when she sat down with her birds. But they wouldn't stay. Jo galloped through my mind instead, and Grandma. Max and Beauty with her big belly. New pictures kept flashing and I couldn't get past them to stay with Mama.

Beach sand. The words from Mrs. Brannigan's jar came to mind. I went into my duffel and took out the small plastic bag of sand and remembered our day at the beach. I saw my tiny white feet in the dark wet sand, Mama on a blanket just out of reach.

Build me a memory.

I'd taken pail after pail of the heavy, wet sand from where the waves fanned out on the shore and built a castle. While I was at it, I rubbed the sand on my arms and in my hair and on my feet so the memory would build into me too.

That sand crept into every crease, deep in my ears and on my scalp, and in the soft spaces between my toes. By the time the castle was done, I was coated up like a cinnamon doughnut. Mama fawned over my droopy castle and told me she wished we could live inside.

Then she took my hand and walked me toward the showers on the slatted wood boardwalk. When I saw where she was headed, I started to fight and kick and cry because I'd gotten it in my head that the memories for the day somehow lived in the sand, and if she washed it off, the day would be gone too. I wanted to bring it home with me, and so Mama took an empty Styrofoam cup and filled it with sand and we put it in the bag so I'd have it forever.

All that lived in the girl on the paper. I put my hand on the other side, on the blank side, feeling torn, wanting to put down my hopes for the future. But that would make it After.

I wasn't sure how much longer I could keep myself in Before.

I stood in front of Grandma's porch, rain gluing the hair to my face, waiting for some direction until I realized I didn't need it. This much I was sure of. I climbed the steps and let myself in the front door. Grandma sat in her sleepless-night chair, knitting something purple.

"Mama wouldn't want me living in a shed," I announced.

She stopped knitting and looked up at me. "Well, it's about time. Let's get you settled in your mother's room."

"Can I sleep on the sofa for now?"

Grandma only paused for a second before going to the closet in the hall and coming back with a pile of sheets and a quilt.

"Let me take that coat," she said. "You're soaked through."

"I'll do it."

I laid Mama's coat on the hearth so it would dry quickly as Grandma made up the couch. I sat on the floor next to the wood stove, trying not to shake, noticing the smell of cleaning. Grandma wrapped a dry quilt around my shoulders and put a towel in my lap.

"Fold your sheets in the morning and set them in that cabinet over there. I don't want to look at a bed in my living room."

As I dried my hair with the towel, Grandma sat on the edge of her rocking chair and watched me.

"The gardening tools you bring every morning in the truck when you drop me off at school, what do you need them for?"

"I spend a few hours every morning in the park, weeding, cutting things back."

"Why didn't you tell me about Mama's fountain when I first got here?"

"I didn't feel much like sharing."

I blinked. She was so honest. Even when it made her look bad. There was something about her honesty that was a comfort, even if the words made me feel prickly. "Tell me about the fountain," I said.

"What do you want to know?"

I shrugged. "Whatever you can tell me."

Grandma's knitting needles moved so fast, I'd never be

able to follow. The fire inside the wood stove threw dancing shadows all over the room.

"She started making birds with your grandpa after a birding trip when she was eight. They'd seen a crane and Anna came home with this story about it being magic. She'd collected some things she'd found while they were out, an old aluminum can, bottle caps, twigs, and some feathers, and she snipped and glued until she had quite the work of art. A set of beautiful wings fixed to a piece of canvas. When she finished your grandfather went on to tell her that the crane wasn't just magic, but that the wings could carry her wishes and sorrows out into the world. So she wrote on a little piece of driftwood that she wished she could fly and attached it to her canvas."

I thought of her wings in my dreams. How I wished I could fly too.

Grandma went on, "By the time she was ten, she worked with a soldering iron and a rivet gun so her birds would be more three-dimensional. But I think the whole reason she built them that way was so she could put her little slips of wishes and sorrows inside. She always hid something in her birds. Did she still do that?"

I nodded.

"Of course," Grandma said. "Her work was beautiful. Thomas encouraged her creativity."

She put her hands to her face and took a couple of deep

and hitching breaths. I stared down at the tiny stitches on the edge of the quilt, not sure what to do. Finally, I got up and grabbed some tissues from the downstairs bathroom. Grandma took them from me, her callused hand giving mine a squeeze. I squeezed back.

Once she'd blown her nose, she picked up where she left off. "Your mama found a book on Central Park and just fell in love with it. The way everyone came together. How you could be alone, but still be with people. She felt her art would fit right in and so that was where the idea came from. To build something where Anna's art would fit right in. I've never been good with words . . ."

Grandma's hands slowed and she stretched the scarf she'd been knitting. She got up and laid it around my neck. "Is this long enough?"

"For me?"

"Of course for you."

I wasn't sure what to say, it was so unexpected, so I nodded.

She unwrapped it from my neck and sat back down, finishing the last stitches. Then she pulled scissors from a small basket that sat beside her and snipped off the end of the yarn. She handed it to me.

"Thank you," I said, and put it on, feeling cozy and warm.

She walked down the hall into Grandpa's office and

came out with a pillowcase stuffed with something that wasn't a pillow. She set it on the floor in front of me and then sat in her rocking chair.

When I paused, she said, "It won't bite."

I reached inside and pulled out the bundle of letters I'd written to Grandma. The ones I'd thrown across the shed before leaving for Mrs. Greene's. I reached in again and pulled out another bundle. More letters. I opened one.

Dear Grace,

I have a great recipe for cherry pie that your mama used to steal right out of the kitchen. That child would hide in the closet and eat half a pie if I wasn't care-ful. First you start with ice-cold water. The crust won't turn out right any other way . . .

I pulled out another and another.

Dear Grace,

I wish you could have sent me your grandparent's letter. I would have loved to answer all your ques-tions about hats and furniture and if I lived where it snowed . . .

She'd answered them all. Twenty-seven letters. Even

the angry ones. She must have done it while I was at Mrs. Greene's.

There was more in the pillowcase: a fluff of purple yarn, some knitting needles, and a book called *Knitting for Beginners*.

"Thank you," I said again, feeling the tears creeping up.

Grandma would never be Mama. But I was starting to think I could love her. Maybe in some future time when it wasn't snowing or raining, and the flowers had grown and then died. Maybe once the leaves turned and the wind started to blow, I might love her. A little.

I waited for the familiar feelings of betrayal and guilt to come knock my door down. But they didn't.

"Sometimes thinking can steal the magic right out of a thing," Grandma said.

I smiled, surprised. "Mama used to say that."

Grandma smiled back and it crinkled her nose. "Did she, now?"

I stared into the crackling fire for a little while wondering how much more of Grandma Mama had brought with her and never told me about, what else I might discover along the way.

"Hop in bed now, it's late. We'll talk more in the morning."

I climbed between the crisp sheets with Jo's earplugs.

She'd told me they had to warm up a bit in order to get soft enough to fit, so I held them tight in my hand. The river was a faint rustle, almost like wind.

I expected Grandma to hurry off to bed, but she stayed in the chair by the fire, knitting something new. As I lay on the sofa in the moonlight, I listened to the lonely sound of Grandma's rocking chair and let the rhythm of it soothe me for a while before putting in the earplugs and going to sleep.

26

One and
the Same

Everything changed three days later when I was doing homework at the breakfast table, staring out the window at the sun slanting through the trees, trying to work a math problem using the Pythagorean theorem, when Grandma's words came back to me.

She always hid something in her birds.

Which, of course, I knew. So why would the fountain be any different?

Grandma was busy at the sink, scrubbing something that probably didn't need to be scrubbed, when I almost shouted, "Did Mama hide something in the fountain?"

She turned around to look at me, wiping her hands on a dish towel. "That's a good question."

I stood up fast, almost knocking the chair over. "Can you take me there?"

"Right now?" Grandma said.

"It's important."

She gave me the once-over. "This wouldn't have anything to do with mischievous raccoons, would it?"

It was a fair question since the only thing separating me from a mischievous raccoon up until now was a coat of fur and a bushy tail. So I didn't get mad. "It's just something I have to do."

With that, Grandma went into the mudroom and put on a sweater instead of her lumberman jacket and grabbed her big black purse.

As we pulled onto Ridge Road, Beauty stood near the fence line and nodded as though wishing me luck.

Grandma barely had the car stopped when I leaped out and started running, kicking up gravel as I went. I wasn't sure what I'd find, but deep down, I knew I was on the right track.

I studied the fountain from every angle, walking around people sprawled on the grass, looking for levers or empty spaces or anything that might be a hiding place. When I didn't see anything obvious, I read the Robert Frost quote on the plaque again.

Where the bird was before it flew,
Where the flower was before it grew,
    Where bird and flower were one and the same.

"It was your mother's favorite poem. She told me it made her think about home." Grandma walked up behind me, dabbing a handkerchief to her brow, just like the one she'd given me all those days ago at Mama's funeral. The sun was just above the tree line, about to fall into leafy shade. "She thought it was a secret, but I knew she put it there for your dad. He was fond of Robert Frost."

"Mama always read it before we moved."

Maybe the poem got her thinking about what home should feel like and so she'd know it once she got there. A thought niggled at me, though, like I was missing something important. I tried hard not to get mad at Mama all over again, telling myself she had no idea she'd be gone so soon, leaving me with a pile of unanswerable questions.

"Where do you think she might have put a hiding place?" Grandma said. She held a hand to her eyes, shading them from the sun. It was the first time I noticed she wore a wedding ring. A plain gold band.

"We can't get inside the metal. So that leaves the rocks. Maybe one of them is loose?"

Grandma started to poke at the rocks and mortar. She went in an orderly line starting at the top and working her way down. I scooted in beside her and did the same thing. A few people watched us from their chairs in the grass. Kids laughed in the distance, flying a parrot kite. A dog barked.

She picked weeds as we went and I did, too, watching

her so I knew the difference between a regular old blade of grass and a weed.

"So you were a ballerina?"

Grandma nodded. "I danced in the San Francisco Ballet. But then I met your grandfather just before he shipped out to Vietnam in 1972 and it changed everything."

"Vietnam! That's ancient history!" I said.

Grandma smiled. "He swept me clear off my pointe shoes, romancing me for two straight weeks before he shipped out. We wrote to each other over the next year and he swore if he made it out alive, he'd marry me.

"It wasn't until he actually showed up at my tiny apartment that I realized he was serious. It was the first and only crazy thing I've ever done in my life. But I just had this deep-down feeling that it was the right thing to do. I gave up dancing to be with your grandfather, and I have never looked back."

I poked and she poked and I thought about love and how it makes you feel clicked open, like a key turned in a lock. Once you knew, you just knew.

"So why didn't you let Mama have that? She loved my dad."

Grandma sat back on the grass and rubbed her forehead, leaving a smudge of dirt. "Sometimes being a mother makes you blind. You think you know what's best and refuse to see any other way."

I tried not to get all worked up again, so I moved away from Grandma to give myself some room. I concentrated on the mineral smell of the fountain water and the crispy softness of a blade of grass. After a few deep breaths, I found a thin gap around a long, flat stone. "I found something!" I shouted. Grandma came over and crouched beside me.

The stone was easy to pull free from the deep opening. Once it was out, we both sat there looking into the darkness of the hole.

"I'll be darned," she said.

I reached in and touched something flat and metal. I pulled out an old, tarnished number 4. I scoured the inside of the opening again, looking for more. Looking for something I might understand.

"What's that?"

I held the number flat on my hand, feeling wobbly all over. "I have no idea."

Once we got back to Grandma's house and she went out to do her gardening, I laid everything out—all my treasure-hunting clues—on the coffee table next to my sofa-bed. Mama's unfinished bird, the postcard of Threads, the map and poem on the back of Mama's flyers, the spoon from the crane in the meadow, and the mysterious number 4.

I slipped the number 4 in my pocket and each of the

other pieces into the Kerr jar with the origami cranes. I tucked the jar behind the sofa and then picked up Robert Frost so I could look over "In a Vale." Something about the poem had stayed with me.

When I got to the stanza that Mama had quoted on her plaque, I realized what it was. She'd left the first two lines off.

Before the last went, heavy with dew,
   Back to the place from which she came—

Where the bird was before it flew,
Where the flower was before it grew,
   Where bird and flower were one and the same.

Mama had read that poem so many times, I almost knew it by heart. Because I'd always been sad when she'd read it, thinking of the move to come, I'd never thought about it having another meaning.

Back to the place from which she came.

She'd recite the poem in the days before we'd leave, over and over again. Those words meant something to her, and while I always took them to mean leaving, now I wondered.

Had she been trying to come home all along?

27

Beginnings

Early Saturday morning, after tossing and turning all night, I finally gave up on sleep, put on boots, and grabbed a flashlight. I left a note for Grandma and walked the trail, eventually finding the meadow, patches of white glowing in the early dusk.

Brand-new daisies.

I settled on the edge of the rocky beach. I couldn't keep away the crushing memories, though, so I tried to tell myself this wasn't really the same river since they had different names. It didn't even look or sound like the same river, and it wouldn't have power over me.

I said this to myself over and over until it turned into a wobbly sort of belief. When the sky finally brightened, I reached in my pocket for the picture of Mama and Daddy, held it by the edges, and walked the meadow in careful circles until I finally came to what looked like the place where they'd posed. It was where the crane now stood, under a taller pine.

The idea that Mama might have been trying to come home had been with me all night, so I went over what I knew. She'd started acting strange when she saw those sandhill cranes migrating home back in February. Quiet, moody, not her usual sunshiny self. Mrs. Greene's words came back to me. *When I tried to ask her why she was leaving, she said she couldn't talk about it, that she might lose her nerve.*

I thought over our last few moves. Each one had gotten us closer and closer to Auburn Valley, with Mrs. Greene's being just an hour away.

So many clues and no answers. I felt like I was going crazy.

I walked over to the crane and rested my ear against the hollow body again. Mama had told me it wasn't the birds with hopes for the future but the ones with sorrows inside that sold more often. People were drawn to them at the local farmers' markets or tiny art festivals we'd sell them in. Those people held them close—their own sorrows scratching at them maybe, itching for a way out—until they'd reach in their pockets and pay whatever Mama was asking. Not that she ever asked for much.

But maybe it wasn't the sorrows people were drawn to, but the idea of letting them go.

"Grace!"

I was about stunned right out of my shoes to see

Grandma at the edge of the meadow. She bent over, out of breath, putting one hand on each knee. "Thank goodness," she gasped. "Come on, it's Beauty. She's having her baby."

"Now?"

"Go on, run ahead. I'll be right behind you."

I shoved the picture back into my pocket and took off at top speed down the trail, through Grandma's garden and the Brannigans' pasture.

Jo was standing just outside the barn door filming me coming toward her. She clicked off as I skidded to a stop, and took my hand.

"I'm so glad you made it in time!" Jo said quietly. She put a finger to her lips and led me to the doorway of the stall. "It'll be any time now."

Beauty turned around a few times and then lay down in the hay, grunting and working to get her baby out while we all stood around the opening and sides of her stall, useless as stumps. Grandma came in the barn eventually and stood behind me. I could feel her there, just a wisp of air between us.

"Push, Beauty, push," Jo whispered.

We all watched, breathless, as one leg worked its way out. Mr. Brannigan went into the stall and pulled on that leg until the next one came, the head down between the knees, all covered in a thick white film. Then he broke the film and cleared it away from the foal's face and nose.

With one last push, the baby was out. A girl. She was mostly white with a few gray splotches, like her mama, and she lay on her side, breathing heavy, as though she'd just run a long way.

"Grace, come here," Mr. Brannigan said.

I walked slowly toward Beauty and the tiny horse that was all legs and knobby knees. Mr. Brannigan told me to kneel right beside the foal.

"Rub her face." He handed me a towel. "That's right. Just like that. And rub your hands along her body and legs."

"She's so warm," I said.

"She needs to know you," he said.

I looked at him, and then at Grandma. With a slight nod of her head, I suddenly realized this little baby thing, this tiny bit of a horse, was mine.

Mine.

I had to sit down for a second and take deep breaths to keep myself from falling all to pieces right there in front of everyone.

A long time went by as the foal moved and was still by turns, eventually thumping around in the hay as she tried to get her legs underneath her. I figured it takes a while to stand on your own for the very first time.

Then Beauty stood, talking in a soft nicker as she licked her new baby. Mr. Brannigan showed me how to take milk from Beauty on my fingers and put them in the foal's mouth. She nursed easily after that and Mr. Brannigan said that's all you can ask for in a new foal.

"What will you name her?" Grandma said.

"Daisy," I said.

"Daisy, hmmmm," Mr. Brannigan said. "That has a good, solid ring to it."

"I like it," Jo said. "Plus, she looks like a daisy."

Grandma nodded as though that made perfect sense.

Because it was Saturday, Jo and I were allowed to stay up as late as we wanted to watch Beauty and Daisy. As long as we didn't interfere with nature taking its course and we did some homework.

"You can count on us, Daddy." Jo gave him a salute.

We hunkered down in the hayloft, which looked in on Beauty's stall. We had all the survival supplies we'd need: beach chairs, a bag of potato chips, two sodas, and my tripod flashlight. I even brought my pad from Mrs. Snickels so I could sketch Daisy.

At dinnertime, Mrs. Brannigan brought out a feast of meat loaf, mashed potatoes, and green beans, with apple pie for dessert, including ice cream.

"Beth called. Again," she said, brow furrowed.

Jo didn't say anything and Mrs. Brannigan shook her head as she left.

"Why don't you want to make up with your friends?" I said.

She shrugged. "They see Max is okay now, with all his hair grown back, and they don't get why I feel like the Other Side is just waiting for us to make one wrong move, change its mind, and take him. They say I'm morbid."

"Is that why you don't want to give him his party?"

"Mom says we'd be tempting fate. Sort of like walking alone at night. Chances are you'll be okay. But there's always a chance you could be murdered by a serial killer. So why risk it?"

"So Max can't have his party because you're afraid of serial killers?" I said.

"Something like that."

"I totally get it."

An hour or so later, Mrs. Brannigan brought out sleeping bags, pillows, and blankets and helped us make a cozy fort for ourselves. She gave us each a forehead kiss and then took our paper plates and trash before climbing down the ladder.

"Max wants to say good night," Mrs. Brannigan said from the stall floor before heading down the driveway toward the house.

"He's going to want to sleep out here with us," Jo said

to me. Her fears about the Other Side taking Max were written there all over her face.

"I don't mind if you don't," I said.

"It's just that sometimes he comes and gets me in the night instead of bothering Mom. She's a little strange if she doesn't get all her sleep. One time, when Max was sick, Daddy opened the coat closet to get a jacket and found her just standing there. She said she was taking a break."

We laughed, even though it really wasn't funny.

"I've got a million of them," she said.

After we stopped laughing, we just sat there for a while, quiet. Beauty lay down and Daisy tucked in the hay beside her.

"Why did you pick the name Daisy?" Jo asked.

Maybe it was the peacefulness of the barn or the fact that I finally had something that truly belonged to me, or maybe it was Jo sharing her worries about Max and her friends, but my usual need to keep things to myself was gone for a second.

"Mama used to tell me this story. Well, it's not really a story, I guess, as much as an idea."

Jo leaned forward, elbows on knees, and gave me her full attention.

"It's silly. Never mind. My mom just really loved daisies."

"No way, Grace. You don't get off that easy." She ticked

off her fingers. "I told you that my brother does an almost constant impersonation of King Tut *before* you found out on your own, that we have the psychic ability to talk to God through our Answer Jars, and that my mother sometimes stands in the closet when she needs a break. You can tell me one silly thing."

I put up my hands in surrender. "Okay, okay! She used to tell me that daisies spoke in a sort of song. A secret hum that birds could feel deep in their bones and it drew them close. There, I told you it was silly."

Jo nodded her head, looking impressed. "That's good. Really good."

And then for some reason we cracked up again. When we were done, we watched Daisy nurse for a while.

"So, I have something to ask you," Jo said. "Is there any way you might get your grandma to give me an interview for the documentary?"

"I can try."

Max appeared in the doorway carrying a sleeping bag and a pillow.

Jo sighed with exasperation. "Come on, Tut. Get on up here," she said.

I think there's a moment in a long stream of moments when you first know someone, and you are finding your way around their quirks, kinks, and general person-ness, that they go from being a new person to a friend. When Jo snuggled her brother into the heavy down of his sleeping bag, then tucked a cowlick of hair into his mummy bandages, all while telling him he was a pain in the butt, I figured that was the moment.

Just like that.

28

A New Sort
of Map

Mama stood on the same slab of rock, waving me toward her, the sandhill cranes by her side. The colorful origami fluttered around her head and she held up the number 4. Her mouth was moving like she was trying to tell me something, but I couldn't hear her over the roar of water. This time, there was no clumsy splashing. I dove straight in. It was icy and stole my breath. The current was strong, and I felt myself going under, sucked down by the swirling water. Soon enough, I didn't know up from down, and I flailed around in a panic, arms and legs banging into rocks and then the sandy bottom. My chest hurt from the pressure of holding my breath, and then my head bumped against something soft. In a panic, I turned to see an arm, white in the murky water, floating beside me.

I woke with a scream caught in my throat, Mama's starfish hand glowing there in the dark.

Trembling, I didn't know where I was until I heard a soft nicker come from the darkness below. Beauty and Daisy. The Brannigan barn. I couldn't turn on the flashlight without waking Jo and Max, so I reached into my duffel and scratched around until my fingers touched the cool metal of the number 4. I wanted to be sure Mama had sent this for me and me alone. I wanted to believe she had parted the heavens and come down to walk the earth, or guided someone else's hand to set this in her secret hiding place for me. That it meant something important because if she didn't leave the clues, if she wasn't behind the origami cranes, then that meant she was gone. Really and truly gone.

I stared straight up into the rafters of the barn and rested it on my forehead, slowing my breaths, hoping meaning might drop into my head and chase everything else away.

I was dog-tired as I sat down to eat breakfast with Grandma the next morning. The table was set just as it always was, latex gloves and everything. Only instead of oatmeal, she'd made pancakes that were warming in the oven.

"How's Beauty doing?" Grandma said.

"She's a good mama."

"And Daisy?"

"Mr. Brannigan told me that every time I'm with her, I'm teaching her. She'll look to me for guidance and I have to be real careful not to give her treats any old time I want or she'll get confused."

When we were done, I cleared the table, and Grandma

scrubbed the dishes. She didn't have a dishwasher in her antique house, so she washed them by hand and set them in a little wooden drainer.

She handed me a soft towel and the dampness brought out the smell of fresh laundry, making me think of my terrible Plan B and how I was glad she was smarter than to fall for any of it.

Grandma showed me where each piece belonged once it was dry, and I felt the maps in my head shift to make room for a new one.

"You've got a lot of work ahead of you," Grandma said. "A horse isn't easy."

"I'm not afraid of work."

"I'll bet you aren't."

When we were done, I hung up the towel. "Thank you. For Daisy."

"You're welcome. Come on. I set something up for you in the living room."

The hardwood floors creaked as Grandma walked me over to the bay window in the front room, where she'd set an old wooden folding table. She'd taken Mama's toolbox from where I'd had it beside the couch and carefully laid out different pieces in a straight line. Brass letters, a glass knob, old metal piping. She set the unfinished crane in the middle of the table. There was epoxy and a small riveting gun.

"The tools used to be your grandpa's," she told me.

I went and fetched the spoons I'd gotten from Margery and then squinted down at the table, running my hands over the tops of all those pieces, waiting for the humming.

But maybe that just wasn't how it was going to work for me.

"I want something from you," I said. Grandma looked at me like she wasn't used to taking demands, but I went ahead anyway. "I want you to do Jo's interview."

She sat down in her sleepless-night chair. There was a fluffed green blanket folded over the back and she took it into her lap, reaching for her knitting. "I suppose I'll have to think about that."

"Why?"

"That park belongs to everyone, not just me. We all have something to say."

"Exactly. But you're the only one not saying anything."

Grandma stopped her knitting. "I suppose the honest answer is I just haven't wanted to think about the past. But maybe it's time."

I worked for part of the afternoon on the crane, went to see Daisy, and then worked on my split-face self-portrait in the evening. I knew Mrs. Snickels had wanted us to spend time thinking about it, but I figured I'd been doing enough thinking for twenty people. And besides, thinking could steal the magic right out of a thing.

I took a swatch from Mrs. Greene's Fabric Wonderland and a price tag from one of Margery's bras. I wrote out the names of all the cities I'd ever lived on little slips of notebook paper and tried to think of what I might have taken from each of those places. A love of garlic from Gilroy; a penny from Pippy in Stockton. I cut out the signature line from one of Lacey's letters (*see that? LOVE*), and pasted everything—the fabric and slips of paper—all around, like destinations on a map. Next to Auburn Valley, I glued down a sketch I'd done of Daisy. There was a small piece of copper wire that I bent into a figure eight and hot-glued, using it as a North, South, East, and West marker. Then I used colored pencils to draw lines of daisies like highways linking everything together.

I left the portrait to dry right out in the open, not even caring when Grandma came down to say good night, her nosy nose leading her to the table to see what I'd been working on.

"You have your mother's flair," she said, and there was no higher compliment.

Grandma must have been sleeping better, because she actually went to bed. I stoked the fire real good, put in my earplugs, and then climbed between the sheets with Daddy's book of Robert Frost. I lay flat on my back and rested the number 4 on my forehead again, hoping for meaning, hoping for the best.

29

Unfolding

I slept without dreams. Without waking up in the night. I felt rested and ready to face the day for the first time in the five weeks I'd been here.

Since it was a school day, I got up when it was still dark and went to the Brannigan barn to check on Daisy. She was up and nursing, and I watched her for a good ten minutes before turning around and heading back to breakfast and Grandma. My heart hurt from love and excitement and grief and it all swirled together in a way that wasn't entirely awful.

When I let myself in the back door, Grandma was fixing tea in her robe and slippers. Her hair wasn't wound into a tight bun yet, and it lay long and wavy down her back.

"You look younger with your hair down like that," I said.

Grandma touched her hair and smiled. "You think

so?" I nodded, and she went on, "Lacey just called. Seems you two didn't talk on Saturday."

"Oh my gosh! I forgot!"

"Go ahead," she said. "Five minutes."

Feeling like a traitor, I went into Grandpa's office and called. She answered on half a ring.

"Where have you been?" she said instead of hello.

As I told her all about Daisy and that I'd seen her born and that she was mine, Lacey got more and more quiet.

"You aren't coming home, are you?" she finally said.

I twisted the phone cord around my finger and thought of a million different things to say so she might not get more upset, but I figured the truth was better. "I don't know."

Or maybe I did, but I just didn't want to tell her.

After a long silence, Lacey said, "Your grandma probably got you the horse so you'll want to stay there. She's trying to trick you. Can't you see that?"

"Trick me how?"

"You're so blind."

"Lacey! Stop talking like that."

"Plus she gets money for taking care of you. Mom said."

I knew Lacey could be selfish, but I'd only seen her mean when someone else poked her first. I was plain flabbergasted.

"Just think about it, Grace. You belong here. With us."

"I've got to go," I said, and hung up.

I couldn't even look at Grandma as she drove me to school, wondering if Lacey might be right. Did she just want me here because she was getting money? I couldn't even stir up the courage to ask her, I was so afraid of the answer.

But Grandma was in a questioning mood. She pelted them at me like she was trying to win something. About Daisy, about needing to sit down with the Brannigans and come up with a plan for Daisy's care and eventually move her into our own barn.

"She shouldn't be without her mother" was all I could say.

Grandma twisted her hands around the steering wheel. "They'll always share a pasture fence, but eventually Daisy will be okay on her own. We'll get her a companion."

I crossed my arms over my chest, clenching my teeth together. I needed to get out of the truck.

"Is something wrong?" she said.

"Just tired."

We pulled up to the curb in front of the school, brakes squeaking. Kids sat on the grass and stood around in groups, laughing and chasing each other as they waited for the bell to ring. Jo waved from her spot next to the front door, waiting for me. Another cloudy day. I was starting to feel like I might suffocate, like I might just shrivel up without sunshine.

"Can I go to the Brannigans' after school?"

"You can do your homework first. Then you can check on Daisy. Spend the evening there if you like."

I climbed out of the truck and slammed the door. When I reached Jo, she took my arm and we walked into school together. I felt tightness climb the back of my throat, but swallowed over it, afraid if I said anything about Grandma, I'd start to cry.

"I need to see Mrs. Turner for a second," I said to Jo. "Go ahead, I'll catch up."

I had to visit the pink crane in Mrs. Turner's office.

"You look like you could use another piece of toast," Mrs. Turner said when she saw me. Her nails were bright red today, each tipped with a white flower.

I picked up the small pink crane that still sat next to her pencil holder on the counter.

"No one came back for it," she said.

My fingers itched to take it, to claim it for myself. The wanting was a physical pain, like a tummy ache, but all over.

"My vote is for secret admirer," I said, wanting to believe it. But I couldn't. Mrs. Turner was right. There was nothing magic about a crane blowing into the office when everyone in the seventh grade had been folding them.

Mrs. Turner touched the place on her chest above her heart. "Do you really think so?"

I nodded, unable to speak.

She plucked the crane out of my hand and replaced it with the chocolate-smeared banana toast.

"Thank you, Grace," Mrs. Turner said, every magical hair in place. "You made my day. Made my day, I tell you."

I rushed out of Mrs. Turner's office and into the bathroom, where I locked myself in a stall and pulled my legs up, crying into my knees. Mr. Flinch was the reason there were cranes floating all over the place. Mama might have left that number 4 in her fountain years ago, or some stranger might have found the secret hiding place and left it for someone else. Either way, it was coincidence, and I started to feel like I was leaning over a cliff, trying to keep Mama from falling, our hands slipping. I closed my eyes and kept hold of her as hard as I could, but she was barely there, hanging on by her fingertips.

Later, in art, Mrs. Snickels laid out our self-portraits on a table at the back of the room with a piece of paper covering the pencil-sketch part, leaving the abstract showing. Each of them was numbered. Mrs. Snickels passed out clipboards and an alphabetical list of names. Whoever could match the most names to their correct abstract would get the Observation of the Month prize.

Beth came to our table snugged in a bright red coat and purple scarf. She said to Jo in a huff, "I hear Beauty foaled over the weekend. You didn't even call me back."

"Why would I call you?" Jo said.

"Because you knew how much I wanted to be there."

"Maybe you should have thought of that before you stopped talking to me."

"I tried to apologize. Besides, you're the one who stopped talking to me first."

Beth took off her jacket. Her T-shirt declared HUGS NOT DRUGS.

Jo took off her jacket. Her T-shirt declared, in black Sharpie, I WENT TO BETH CRINKLE'S HOUSE AND ALL I GOT WAS THIS STUPID T-SHIRT.

Beth stood there, stunned.

Then she laughed.

Then Jo laughed.

And it was over, just like that.

Beth pulled up an extra stool and they giggled quietly as the other kids in class filed by the table of self-portraits one by one. They gushed and talked about all the little things they'd missed over the last couple of weeks. I watched Beth and Jo finish each other's sentences and how they each fluttered their hands the same way as they talked and was filled with anger and frustration. They'd been friends for life. I was brand-new. Jo had probably just been nice because I was momless and she was on the outs with her own friends. As soon as they kissed and made up, I'd get booted to the curb. It had happened before.

Mrs. Snickels called us for our turn at the self-portrait table.

"I always win these," Jo informed me as she inspected, her nose two inches from each portrait. I moved away from her as Beth and Ginger nudged in between us.

"It's because you used to watch so much *Scooby-Doo*," Beth said. "You're a natural at solving mysteries. Remember that time . . ."

I tuned them out, surprised at how many portraits I seemed to recognize. Jo had a strip of photo negative on hers. Archer had a drawing of a ladle. Beth Crinkle's was the easiest of all; the entire abstract side was filled with tiny slogans.

Someone came up behind me and whispered, "That one's yours. The one with the figure eight."

Archer stood beside me, a bit red in the face. He met my eyes, though, and didn't look away.

"How did you know?" I whispered back.

He traced a figure eight onto the top of my hand and shrugged with a smile.

It wasn't possible for him to turn redder without bursting something. He moved past me down the line of portraits and then took a seat. Stubbie nudged him in the shoulder and made smoochy noises. Mrs. Snickels walked over and feather-dusted Stubbie until he stopped.

I didn't leave Mr. Flinch's classroom when everyone else filed out for lunch. I wasn't entirely sure why, aside from the fact that I didn't much feel like sitting in the cafeteria while Jo and Beth and Ginger became a team again.

"Do you have a question, Grace?" Mr. Flinch said as he went about adjusting the blinds against the sun. I wondered what he'd wear once the weather turned too warm for elbow-patch sweaters. He wore a plain tan one today.

"Can you show me how to fold an origami crane?" I asked.

"Of course!"

Mr. Flinch went into his desk and brought out two fancy sheets of gold paper. He handed me one and kept the other. His fingers were long and graceful as he began. I followed him fold for fold.

"I have a question about Sadako," I said.

"Yes?"

"It's just that, what difference did any of it make? She worked so hard, and she just died anyway. She never got her wish."

He thought about that for a minute.

"I think folding cranes was a way to hold on to herself, and to life. We all have to find a way to cope."

Death is a hard nut to crack, Mrs. Greene had said, and it scared me to think I'd made the whole thing up, the signs, that Mama was trying to tell me something. It was just some crazy idea to help me get through the grief of losing Mama. I thought of Max's entombment party, Mrs. Brannigan and her Answer Jars, my friend Timmy and his imaginary friend Wrinkle, and a thousand paper cranes. How sometimes it took crazy to get to normal.

Then I thought about how this whole thing started: with an unfinished crane in a toolbox that Grandma gave me.

Grandma.

We folded in silence until our cranes were done. He set his down on my desk and I set mine next to his.

"How do you know when you're ready to stop?" I said.

"You just know."

30

The Secret Hum
of a Daisy

Jo found me at my locker after school. "Where did you disappear to at lunch? I wanted you to tell everyone about Daisy being born. Plus they wanted to know how you came up with the name and I sort of thought that was private, so I didn't tell."

"You were there when she was born. Why didn't you tell them yourself?"

"She's your horse. Plus you would have told it better."

"How do you know?"

"Are you mad about something?"

I got busy shoving books and notebooks into my backpack. "No. Yes. I don't know."

Jo put her hand on my arm. "What's wrong?"

I worked hard to push the words out. "Where will I fit now that you and Beth and Ginger are friends again?"

Jo shrugged. "Right here with us, I guess. You're not all that special, you know." But she said it with a smile.

So I smiled too. "Thanks for not telling."

"Come on. And no pouting. Beth is coming and we don't want to get her going with her slogans. Once she gets going, she doesn't stop."

It was sprinkling when Grandma picked me up from school.

"Will you take me to the cemetery?" I asked. I figured it was time to check on Mama, to see my father's grave. Maybe I would know what to think about everything once I was there with them. All together.

Grandma only hesitated a beat. "Of course."

When she parked in the small cemetery lot, I thought of Mama's funeral. How so much had changed in the six weeks since she died. I wondered what had happened to the girl who moved in all those days ago. If I would miss her.

We stopped at Mama's grave first. It had been perfectly maintained. Swept of leaves and weeds, flowers planted, dust brushed off her headstone. I thought about Grandma wearing her gardening uniform every morning when she dropped me off at school.

"You've been coming here too," I said.

She nodded and then plucked a tiny weed that was growing up alongside Mama's name. Grandpa's headstone was right beside hers. The cemetery grass was lush and green.

"I like to think they're together somewhere," Grandma said.

I looked into the sky, the clouds thinning and pulling apart, reminding me of eating cotton candy. The drizzle was gone and the sun peeked out.

"Do you believe in heaven?" I asked.

"I do."

"Just like that?"

She thought it over. "Yes."

"What does it look like?"

"I don't know. My idea of it changes." Grandma took a small soft-bristled clean-up brush out of her purse and swept some dust off Grandpa's headstone.

"So there's not a blueprint somewhere?"

Grandma smiled. "Some people believe there's a blueprint. But I like to think that God, or whoever is in charge, doesn't dabble in blueprints."

I borrowed Grandma's brush and cleaned off Mama's headstone, tracing my finger along the crane I'd chosen, carved into the stone.

"Do you get paid for having me live with you?"

"Who told you that?" Grandma said, startled. She touched the cross at her neck.

"Lacey."

She took a Safeway plastic grocery bag out of her black

purse and tossed the weeds into it. "Lacey misses you. Wants you to come back."

"She does."

Grandma was quiet, maybe letting that idea sink in.

"I get money every month from your mama's social security. It's not much, but it's going into a bank account for your college education."

"So you're not taking care of me for the money?"

"I'd have taken you if I had to *pay* money."

That made me smile.

After we'd spent some time with Mama, I asked Grandma to take me to my father's grave. She walked me to a small area shaded by oaks, a white picket fence just a few feet away.

"His parents are here. Margery had them all buried together."

A poem was engraved on the family headstone.

A solitary bird, hollow it flew
Through a haze of months marked by the moon
Come to a meadow, shiny with dew
Where hollow bones sang, and deep inside grew
The secret hum of a daisy in June.

"Your mama picked it. Scott was such a wonderful writer."

Of course. Daddy had written the poem, not Mama. I kneeled down and laid my cheek against the stone. My birthday was in June. Maybe I was the daisy, which would have made Mama the meadow and Daddy the solitary bird. We fit together like a puzzle.

I turned to look at Grandma. Her hair was still loose, and it floated around her face and down her back. She got out her clean-up brush again and swept Daddy's family grave while I took the number 4 out of my pocket.

"It was you, wasn't it? You set the clues."

I so wanted her to give me a puzzled look and tell me she didn't know what I was talking about.

"Your grandfather used to leave little treasure hunts for your mama when he'd go overnight on cabinet installs. I'd get her to follow it when Thomas was on his way back home. I didn't know if she did treasure hunts with you or not, but I figured I'd give it a try."

I wanted to yell at her. To tell her that she tricked me and I'd never trust her. I had to sit down for a minute and let it all sink in. Right there in the wet grass.

"Did anyone else know?"

"They were all there if you needed them. Lou and Mel, Margery, Sheriff Bergum."

So there had been help along the way, just like there'd always been with Mama. I just didn't know it.

"What does the number four mean?"

"Do you really want me to give you the answer?"

I thought it over and sighed. "I suppose not."

Grandma shrugged. "I didn't know what else to do."

"You're the grandma; you should have known." Even as I said it, I realized that sometimes people did what they could, not what they should, and I didn't think that was reason enough to be mad.

Whatever magic there'd been was gone. I felt it fly off, like Mama kept doing in my dreams.

After spending some time with Daisy, there was a lot to think about that night as I read through every last page in my father's writing folder, so much of it reminding me of Robert Frost. Daddy didn't shy away from the sadness in things the way Mama did, and that's when I understood there were two kinds of beauty. One you recognized with your eye, like watching a new horse being born, and one you recognized with some deep place inside yourself that was hurting. Mama drifted toward the first, and Daddy the second, and together, they made me.

After a while, I tinkered with Mama's unfinished crane. When I couldn't make any of the pieces work, I got up to pace, tired of my own deep-down hurting, the deep, hard scratching that wouldn't stop.

Writing would help me through it, just like it always had. And where I used to think that writing was like the little hole in a teakettle to let out steam, I figured it was more than that. I hoped the hundreds, thousands, maybe millions of words I wrote down would help me fill the empty place left by Mama and make me whole.

I picked up Mrs. Snickels's sketchbook and flipped to a blank page in the middle, trying to ignore my feeling that I was about to change everything by writing down something about After. But I couldn't keep it locked up anymore.

I took a pencil and let the words come. All those words about Mama and the night she died that I'd been stuffing down. When they were all out, I folded that piece of paper into a tight square and shoved it in my pocket.

That was how I saved myself.

31

World Peace

The dream was familiar. Though, this time, Mama wasn't sitting on the slab of rock in the middle of the river. She sat cross-legged on the short, rocky beach, wings spread wide. The cranes were there on the bank, the way they had been the morning she died. She reached her hand out to me, but no matter how many steps I took, I couldn't get to her.

Eventually, she stood up and walked toward me. Taking my hand, she led me back to her rocky perch and we sat side by side, watching the pale yellow sun rise over the hills in the distance.

The birds came then. All those metal birds she'd put together over the course of my life. Origami cranes too. They flew around her and off into the sky, the brightness of morning shining off their wings. I held on to Mama. Tight. Feeling the coolness of her hand, memorizing it.

And then she was gone, up and away, following her birds.

I woke up, unsure of where I was. I stared at the ceiling, counting deep breaths, remembering I was at Jo's. Sleeping on her dusty trundle. The baby monitor next to my head so we could hear Daisy. A compromise Mrs. Brannigan came up with when she caught Jo and me sneaking out in the middle of the night.

After my breathing was under control, I noticed the door was ajar, a dim light coming through. Jo wasn't in bed.

I walked quietly down the hall toward the light coming from Max's room and stood outside his usually closed-tight door, scared at what I'd find.

I pushed the door open with one finger. Max stood to the side of his bed, and Jo was wrapping him with more bandages. They didn't notice me.

"That's good," Max whispered.

"No way you'll come unwrapped again," Jo said.

And then my eye was drawn upward toward his high ceiling, where hundreds of origami cranes hung down like twinkling stars. Jo and Max looked toward the door.

"I'm sorry, Grace, we didn't mean to wake you," Jo said as she pulled the bandages tighter. Max looked straight at me.

When Jo finished, Max climbed into bed. She sat down beside him, humming softly. After a minute, she got up and came toward the door.

"Grace," Max said.

"It's late," Jo said.

"Just for a minute."

"Oh, all right," Jo said. "I'll be downstairs."

I took Jo's place on the edge of Max's bed.

"Jo doesn't like to face things," he said. "It's better to face things. That's what Mom says. Don't try and make stuff up, and don't ignore it. Face it."

He set a crane in my hand.

I looked at the crane sitting there on my palm, like I had that first day of school, letting myself think of Mama, of sitting on the porch at Mrs. Greene's and watching the cranes fly home.

"Why did you leave them for me?"

He shrugged his little mummy shoulders. "I left them for lots of people. I figured you all needed them more than I did."

"My first day of school was better because of you," I said.

Max smiled. Or, at least, I thought he did. His bandages moved up. "Why?"

"That was when I found the silver crane in the church bushes."

"I didn't do that. I snuck one into Mr. Flinch's class. The one made from newspaper."

"The little silver one. Looked like it was made out of a gum wrapper, only bigger?"

"Nope. Don't even remember one like that. I take them down from my ceiling one by one. Jo made them for me."

"Are you sure?"

"Of course I'm sure," Max said. And with that, he scooched under the covers and closed his eyes. He was breathing deep and steady in no time.

I figured the first-day-of-school crane must have been Grandma's doing as I went downstairs, and decided to ask her about it later. There was a dim night-light shaped like a horse plugged into the wall in the kitchen. Jo was busy fixing hot chocolate, her short hair sticking straight up on one side. I pulled out a chair and sat down, setting the baby monitor on the kitchen table.

"I knew about Sadako's cranes from Mr. Flinch's project. When Max was sick, it seemed like something I could do instead of just sit around waiting," Jo said.

She poured the chocolate into two mugs and sat down across from me. "At first Max didn't respond to the treatments, but by the time I'd finished the thousand, he was getting better, so I couldn't stop, because then what would happen? There are two Hefty bags full out in the garage. Every day I have to fold a crane."

"He needs that entombment party."

"You know why we won't do that."

I nodded. "I think he wants to be prepared. For everything."

"I don't want him to be prepared. I want him to keep fighting."

"He can do both."

She pushed her chocolate away. "Is a party supposed to make it easier?"

"I don't think it's about easy or hard. It's about what Max needs to get through it for himself. You and Sadako have your cranes, and Max has his entombment party."

And I had Mama's signs, even though I made them up. Jo was quiet. We all did weird things to get us through it. The trick seemed to be figuring out when to stop.

"Let's consult the jars," Mrs. Brannigan said out of the shadows.

She walked over to the bookshelf in the living room and closed her eyes, running her hands through the air. She grabbed a misshapen pottery jar with a wide cork lid.

"Mom, this isn't the time to find out where your keys were last Tuesday or how to make grandma's rhubarb pie," Jo said.

Mrs. Brannigan sat down next to Jo and set the jar on the table. "It's not always about what I pull out of the jar.

It's about reminding myself that I've been lost before, and found a way through it."

She pushed the jar toward me. "Let's see what you pull out."

I looked at the jar for a long time thinking of my beach sand before reaching inside and closing my hand around what felt like the right one.

I carefully unfolded the paper and read, "'Rasputin.'"

"See?" Jo said, but she was smiling.

She dug around in the jar and fished out a piece of yellow lined paper. *Albert Einstein*, it said.

"Maybe Grace is right about the party, Mom. Besides, it's what Einstein would want," Jo said, and we tried to laugh quietly.

"How can I argue with Einstein?" Mrs. Brannigan said. She pulled out *Grilled Cheese, Six Months,* and *Mississippi.*

In five minutes, we were giggling loud enough to bring Mr. Brannigan down the stairs, hair sticking up seven different ways. "Did you find the answer to world peace?"

World peace, I tell you.

32

Mummies Rock!

Sheriff Bergum showed up with some men on his day off. It was still strange to see him in a regular old long-sleeved shirt and jeans. They went to work restoring the barn. I sat on a nearby boulder under a tree and watched. Eventually, Sheriff Bergum saw me sitting there and called me over. He put a hammer in my hands and I helped them nail and carry lumber, put up ladders, and broom away the cobwebs.

When I wasn't at the Brannigans' tending to Daisy, or thinking about what the number 4 might mean, I worked on Mama's unfinished crane. Try as I might, I couldn't get the wings right. I tried spoon bowls, the broken pieces of a vegetable steamer, and even real-life feathers I'd found in the meadow, but none of them worked. I'd know when I found the right piece, though. Mama had always told me that good art was about knowing what to keep and what to leave behind, and I tried to do that inside myself too.

It was finally time for the long-awaited entombment party. Jo answered the door, a strained look on her face. Stepping into her house, I could see why. The smoke detector was going off and Mrs. Brannigan was running around the living room, waving a giant broom, yelling, "Burnt weenies!" Mr. Brannigan leaned back in a huge brown Barcalounger, a cowboy hat pulled low over his eyes as though he was sleeping, with mummified Max nestled in his lap.

Mrs. Brannigan whacked Mr. Brannigan on his slippered foot, screeching, "The humidifier! Get the humidifier!"

Mr. Brannigan turned up the volume on his baseball game. The fans went wild.

As Grandma and I watched from the doorway, Mrs. Brannigan made a complicated hand gesture that looked like a cross between warding off the evil eye and throwing imaginary salt over her shoulder.

"Maybe we should go to your house," Jo said.

"Good heavens! Mrs. Jessup! I didn't see you there," Mrs. Brannigan said. She pawed at a wisp of hair that had fallen from her short ponytail and set the broom against the wall. She whacked Mr. Brannigan again on his foot with the flat of her hand.

Sheriff Bergum came from the kitchen holding a

handful of weedy-looking mustard greens. He took off his hat and started to hand it to Grandma, then he snatched his hat back and held out the mustard greens instead.

"That was kind of you, Pete."

"Let's get those in some water," Mrs. Brannigan said, and before Grandma could take them, she bustled the flowers right out of Sheriff Bergum's hand. He stood there for a second with his hat still over his heart and his empty bouquet hand out like he didn't know what hit him. He put his hat back on.

I put two fingers up to my eyes and pointed them at him. He laughed.

More guests came. Ginger and Beth were there with a gaggle of Max's friends, including Spencer, the friend he blamed for hiding his red suitcase. Lou and Mel came with a banana cream pie and a pot full of corn chowder to satisfy Max's need for all things yellow. Margery brought something in a bag that made Mrs. Brannigan blush. Archer came with Stubbie. Beth even came prepared with a speech and T-shirts for everyone that said MUMMIES ROCK!

Mrs. Brannigan shooed us out with her giant broom so we could take in the vitamin D she thought we desperately needed after a long winter. The broom being almost as big as she was. And there on the deck, beside the smoking barbecue, was a roughly carved sarcophagus, something

292

I learned Sheriff Bergum had been working on with Max for weeks. Max scampered over and climbed in. Jo was attaching her camera so she could film the whole thing.

The TV switched off but Mr. Brannigan didn't get out of his big chair. After standing around a bit awkwardly waiting for him, Mrs. Brannigan hurried back inside. Only instead of whacking Mr. Brannigan with her broom, she rested a tender hand on the sleeve of his plaid shirt. He brushed a hand at his eyes as he walked toward us.

Jo stood at the makeshift podium Mrs. Brannigan set up using a stool from their kitchen island. She cleared her throat and said just the right words, which Max had helped her with.

"Here lies Max. Brother, son, and friend. He loved everything yellow because he thought yellow was the happiest color. He did not like comic book superheroes because he thought they were fake. He loved his mother because she gave him raspberry tea when he was sick all night and told him the angels were taking his hair so they could weave golden patches for their wings. He loved his sister because she shaved her head when the angels took his hair, and she folded cranes until her fingers were stiff with paper cuts. He loved his father because he'd fall asleep by his bed under his cowboy hat. Real superheroes wear cowboy hats, in case anyone was wondering how to tell. And last, but not least, he loved Grace because she was brave and being brave is catching. Sort of like chicken pox, only in a good way."

Throats cleared. Birds chirped in the trees. I pulled out Mr. Flinch's "dramatic flair" handkerchief.

Sheriff Bergum stood up, nearly knocking over the folding chair he'd been sitting in. Grandma helped him right it. "Max Brannigan was a pain in the rear end."

Everyone laughed. Sheriff Bergum reached in the pocket of his jeans and took out a childish drawing of a sarcophagus. "This was his idea of a good set of plans." Everyone laughed again.

"May the sarcophagus protect him in the afterlife."

He sat down, crossing his long legs and pulling on the lid of his black cowboy hat.

Beth Crinkle stood up and read a list: *Top Ten Reasons to Love Max Brannigan*. Ginger quoted Shakespeare.

Mrs. Brannigan read a letter she'd written to Max one night in the hospital. He'd gotten an infection after his first round of chemo and they thought he might not make it. The letter talked about how lucky she was to be his mother and that she was so glad to have known him. That he'd changed her life forever. Mr. Brannigan didn't say a word, couldn't maybe, and instead set his cowboy hat on top of Max, who was lying still, eyes closed, hands clasped to his chest.

There were a lot of cowboy hats in this place.

Stubbie stood up and pushed a button on a CD player. I wondered if he was going to try and do a stand-up routine, but instead, I heard the chords leading to "Amazing Grace." He sang in a clear and beautiful voice, which made me feel two parts awe and one part giggly. I had to bite my lips to keep the giggly part from happening.

As he sang, everyone took turns laying something precious in Max's tomb. I put one of Mama's spoons so that he'd always be able to eat good soup. Archer laid a folded napkin on his chest and I wondered what Ladle Boy was up to. Lou placed in a recipe card for corn chowder, and Mel put in his famous wooden ladle. I'd helped Grandma make a lemon cake, and she set the box down into the sarcophagus. When Stubbie was finished, he laid a small fishing pole next to the ladle.

In the end, Mr. Brannigan sealed him up.

The smell of the barbecue must have gotten to Max, though, because he insisted, from inside the sarcophagus, that we forgot the most important part. How was he supposed to go to the afterlife without a good meal?

So not only did Max assure himself of a wonderful afterlife, but I got some proof of magic. I went around asking who might have left that little origami crane in the bushes on my first day of school. Archer? Jo? Grandma?

But no one knew.

As Lou ladled corn chowder into plastic King Tut

bowls, I thought maybe heaven wasn't only in the great big sky with comfy furniture and fireplaces. I figured it lived in small places too, like a bowl of good soup or the folds of an origami crane.

With the ceremony over, and Max prepared for the afterlife, Jo and I decided to check on Daisy.

I knew something was wrong as soon as I walked into the barn. The horses were all restless in their stalls, snorting and stomping.

We found Daisy lying on her side, breathing fast, covered in sweat. I put a hand on her belly. "What's wrong with her?"

But Jo was already gone, yelling across the field for her dad to hurry.

Mr. Brannigan ran in first, Mrs. Brannigan on his heels. He checked Daisy's eyes and pressed on her gums. He laid a hand and then his ear to her belly. He tried to stand her up, but she wasn't having any of it. Mrs. Brannigan led a resistant Beauty to the stall next door.

Frantic, I said again, "What's wrong?"

"I believe it's colic," Mr. Brannigan said.

"What's colic?" I said, panic rising. Mrs. Brannigan came over and stroked Daisy's head. Daisy moaned a little under her touch.

"Colic is when the intestines get into a bit of a twist," she said.

"How serious is that?"

"Let's wait until the vet comes. There's no use in getting alarmed right now," Mrs. Brannigan said.

Mr. Brannigan tried to get Daisy standing by soothing and whispering. He touched and coaxed while Beauty whinnied next door. Daisy rolled on her back, onto her other side, and eased up. She stood on wobbly legs, like she did the day she was born.

I held back, afraid to move. Mrs. Brannigan touched my shoulder. "Walk her around. That'll help."

Daisy nodded her head up and down, up and down, as if in agreement.

I walked over to Daisy and whispered soothing words. "You can do it. You are brave and you are loved."

Jo came up beside me and took my hand. She led me out into the pasture, where Daisy nipped at her flanks and wanted to walk in tight circles. She tried to lie down again, but we didn't let her.

After what felt like an eternity, a white truck came barreling down the driveway, and Dr. Wilson ran across the field. He had round glasses and a tightly trimmed mustache and beard. He called us back into the barn, where he took Daisy's vitals and gave her a quick shot. He reached into his bag and pulled out a long hose. His hands looked soft and sure.

"Thatta girl," he said.

Mr. Brannigan kneeled down and held Daisy's head as Dr. Wilson slid the hose into her nostril, slow and gentle. He kept feeding it down until I was sure it would come out her backside. Then he took a large container of liquid and poured it into the hose. She didn't much care for that. Beauty was still agitated in the stall next door, snorting and nodding her head.

"This is mineral oil. We need to get it into Daisy's stomach to help her break things up," he said to me.

"Is she going to be okay?" I said.

Dr. Wilson didn't answer. He looked at Mr. Brannigan, who had stood up, hands shoved in his front jeans pockets.

"It's serious, Grace," Mr. Brannigan said.

Once the oil was down, Dr. Wilson took to rubbing her stomach. "Do this every half hour or so. In between rubbings, keep her walking. Can you two do that for me?"

Jo and I nodded.

"We'll all help," Grandma said, and I had to take a deep breath to keep from falling down.

Jo and I took Daisy out into the pasture and walked with her. The afternoon wore on to night. Everyone tried to take over for us, but Jo and I wouldn't let her go, so they took turns walking alongside. Beth and Ginger, the Brannigans, Margery, Archer and Stubbie, Lou and Mel. Grandma brought us more hot dogs around dinnertime, which we couldn't eat. At some point, Mr. Brannigan came out with lanterns and set them on the outside of the barn and hung one in the tree in the pasture. It was enough to keep us from stumbling. He lit a fire in the fire pit, where everyone took turns keeping warm. Lou wrapped us each in a soft blanket.

Archer and Stubbie walked with us, their heads down, hands shoved in pockets. I was glad for the company.

As we walked Daisy around in circles, wondering if she'd make it, I thought about Mama's last night. Where Mrs. Greene lived in Hood really wasn't much more than a couple shakes of houses with a sprinkling of dust and a big dollop of flat asphalt connecting one thing to another. Like the yellow brick road, only it wasn't yellow or brick, and it didn't lead anywhere special. A dusty town full of small animals that were always getting themselves smashed to a pulp along the asphalt road.

So I decided we needed a dog. What with so many of them dead along the side of the road or wandering around the dusty fields without collars, grungy and electrified with hunger. Mostly to save it from whatever fate was sure to come down the freeway. And only a little bit to save myself.

Mama was firm on the no-pets rule. We went round and round over it. A pet would make it harder for us to move. A pet would be one more mouth to feed. A pet needed a home it could count on.

"What about me? Maybe I need a home I can count on!"

With that, I'd slammed out the door and stomped down the asphalt road. Mama followed, keeping her distance. And because I couldn't stay mad for long, I slowed down. Eventually, her warm hand took mine.

"I'm sorry, Grace," she'd said. "But we're leaving and we can't take a dog."

I didn't say anything right away. Mostly out of my own shock that I'd finally said something out loud about not wanting to go. Something I'd been carrying around in a secret pocket of my heart for as long as I could remember. Maybe secret pockets were only good for so long, though, and eventually the secret had to make its way out or rot there like fish in a bucket.

"I'm not going anywhere, Mama," I said, and took my hand from hers.

Mama looked so sad. Like I'd broken her heart right there on the asphalt road. Broken it into a million pieces. I almost took it back. But I didn't.

It was dusk, the sun going down pink and gray. "Mrs.

Greene has dinner on the table," she said. And so we went back, side by side, and ate dinner.

Later, when she wanted to climb into bed with me to read Robert Frost, I told her I was tired and turned my back. So she went for a walk instead.

I looked up into the night sky, the stars twinkling bright, Jo walking beside me. It wasn't my fault I wanted to stay in one place. It wasn't my fault we'd fought about it that last night and that she'd gone for a walk.

It wasn't my fault that I wanted to stay here with Grandma even though I was scared.

"I won't leave," I said to Daisy. "I'll never leave you, no matter what."

33

The Number 4

I never thought I could be so happy to see a horse shoot manure. We'd kept walking with Daisy until around three in the morning. When she cleared out, everyone gave a great whoop and danced around the fire pit. Mr. Brannigan declared Daisy out of the woods. He took a turn walking her around, which was the last thing I remembered before falling into a deep sleep in the hay of her stall.

It was still dark when I woke up with an image of the number 4 sitting in front of me, almost real enough to touch, and the memory of where that number 4 came from.

Just like that.

It was barely light enough to see as I tiptoed past Grandma snoozing on a cot next to the stall, and ran into the pasture and down the trail. Mama's treasure hunts always started with a bird and ended on the porch of whatever place we were living in. When Grandma had driven me to her house for the very first time, there'd been a number missing from her porch. The number 4.

It was irrational to believe that Mama might be there somehow, like she always had been, but I couldn't help it. Even though I knew Grandma set the clues, even though I knew Mama was gone, sometimes believing something didn't make any kind of rational sense. Heck, there weren't any blueprints of heaven, either, but people believed in it. Believed hard.

I rounded the last corner and came up the side of the house to the front.

The porch was empty. Of course it was empty.

I slumped onto the stairs and eventually let the shakes take over and the hitching sobs rack my whole self, a tsunami and an earthquake rolled into one. Mama was gone and she was never coming back. And now I had to take a chance on someone new.

At some point in all that, Grandma appeared beside me and sat quiet and still.

Eventually, the sobs tapered off. I took the number 4 out of my pocket again, and this time, she took it into her long, graceful hands, holding it the way you might hold something precious.

"Two days before you got here, it fell off the porch and brought to mind your grandfather's treasure hunts. Call me silly, but I took that falling porch number as a sign."

"I believe in signs," I whispered.

She took my hand.

"I'm sorry," Grandma said, "for so many things." And the words meant something in a way they wouldn't have just two weeks ago. Maybe everything in this life worked or didn't work according to where you were standing at any given moment. A building could fall on your head or you could accept an apology. Two steps to the left and it might never happen.

We sat alongside each other, the way Mama and she must have done hundreds of times here and there in all the corners of their life. There was love—even if Grandma wasn't good at showing it—and lots of ordinary. There probably wasn't much worrying over more than the day's events. Then Mama sat at the scene of a terrible accident, Daddy's head in her lap, maybe, or her own father's, and everything went skyrocketing off in a different direction after that.

"How do I know you won't turn your back on me one day?" I said.

Grandma took my chin in her hand and looked me straight in the eye. "Because I won't."

Margery had talked about a cavernous space and how it can grow between people. It was so easy to stay on your side of that space instead of wading through all that emptiness and loneliness, making a thousand wrong turns. But

Grandma had headed out into it anyway. By answering my letters, even the angry ones, and telling me the truth about things. Grandma walked out to meet me halfway and maybe that was enough.

But I had to do my part. And even though I was scared of a million different things, of losing everything again, I did it by reaching in my pocket and giving her the poem I'd written.

Three a.m.
the house empty of Mama's breathing.
She'd gone for a walk
because that's what she did when sleep wouldn't come
and poems didn't work
and her daughter was too full of anger
to help her.
So I walked outside where the cold stung my nose
and breath took its own shape
and through that shape
was a different one
in the water.

They say time slows when something awful happens
That is true.
It took an infinity to reach her
and see that she'd slipped

hit her head
and landed facedown
instead of faceup.
Such a small difference
in direction.
I took a flowered sheet off the bed,
pulled her onto the bank,
covered us both.
Mrs. Greene found us hours later
but I wouldn't leave Mama
until the police came and pulled me off.
I would have climbed into the casket too
but there wasn't room
for both of us.

Grandma took me into her arms then. They were hard with muscle, strong and warm. We sat there together, watching the sky turn blue, for a very long time.

34

Possibility

Dear Lacey,

I know you're mad at me. I know you want me to come back. But I finally feel like I'm where I'm supposed to be, and I hope you can forgive me sometime soon so we can keep talking about the evil Marsha Trett with her beef tongue adventures and whether or not Denny comes to his senses, and of course, how Jill and Carrie are working out. I'm only a little over an hour away and Grandma says she'll drive me once a month, so we can see each other. I think I might have even talked Grandma into buying a computer since I could use it for homework. We could e-mail every day.

Archer asked me to "attend" the premier of Jo's movie that I told you about. That was actually how he said it, "Grace, will you attend Jo's premiere with me?" I told him yes. But only if he agreed to bring the popcorn and stop using words like "attend."

I'm in the movie, and so is Grandma. Jo filmed

Daisy being born and asked if she could use it. At first I said no, but then the idea of being part of things finally grew on me. So I changed my mind.

Grandma finally let Jo interview her, even though she didn't talk a whole lot. What she said was important, though. She said she didn't think much about it at the time, what kind of place the park would be for everyone. She just put it together one piece at a time and watched as everyone else did too. She also said she didn't go much when Grandpa was alive and Mama was home. But once they were gone, she went there to remember. She planted and weeded and kept things beautiful as an apology, she said, and as a way to work out her sorrow. Mama can see it all, I believe. From her place in heaven.

Grandma said she gave the interview for me because she wants me to have the whole story about things from now on.

Daisy is getting bigger every day. She likes peanut butter and lemon Popsicles. I hope you and your mom will come to the premiere so you can meet everyone. It would mean a lot to me.

Send me some bad poems. I love you.

Grace

· · ·

Max didn't need his bandages after the entombment party. He turned himself into a cowboy superhero and took to wearing a zebra-striped cloak Margery had fashioned out of a winter robe off the sale rack. Plus Mr. Brannigan's cowboy hat. Jo and I laughed at what "normal" looks like sometimes.

I ended up telling Jo everything. All about the clues and the treasure hunt and how I believed it had been Mama. It felt good to tell someone and I expected her to laugh or look uncomfortable, but instead, she had given me a hug and told me I was one of a kind, and since we never did figure out who left that silvery crane in the bushes on my first day of school, we both liked to think it might have been Mama, that maybe no one is ever really gone, they're just . . . somewhere else.

Mama didn't come back to me in my sleep, even though I missed her something awful. The rain stopped coming down. Margery's summer shipment arrived, and Jo and I helped her sort bras for a whole day while we listened to sad country music and ate cookies. Grandma and I re-attached the missing number 4 to the porch.

Lou sewed a bunch of white sheets together and draped it over the side of Spoons, and Jo had her premiere of *It's a Wonderful Small-Town Life* for her final project in art.

The whole town showed up with lounge chairs and picnic blankets and settled into the parking lot next door. Mrs. Greene and Lacey didn't come to the premiere, which broke my heart a little, but Lacey just needed more time. And I wasn't going to hold that against her. We all needed different bits of time.

Grandma bought a photo album and we filled it with what was left of Mama's childhood pictures from the attic, plus I added some from my own albums. Christmases and birthdays. A father who loved her. A mother who loved her too. It was like Grandma and me coming together was the only way to make Mama a whole person. And so we did that, little by little, in all the ways we could.

I asked Grandma if she thought Mama might have been coming home, but Grandma didn't know either. The only other clue I'd found was when I took out Mama's old AAA map of California, the one she used to pop with a pinhole for the next town along the way. As I held it up to the light one day, I saw that the pinholes glowed a pattern, moving up the state of California in a steady line, which made me wonder again if Mama was migrating home like the sandhill cranes, only one small step at a time. I supposed I'd never know, but my gut, which was getting stronger by the day, told me it was true.

I moved into Mama's room. The first thing I did was

paint the walls "Faraway Sky," this awesome purple color. Then I nailed a bulletin board to the wall and pegged up random pictures. Mama and Daddy. Margery. Mrs. Greene and Lacey. Beauty and Daisy. Jo and Max. Archer, Stubbie, Beth and Ginger. The Brannigans. Lou and Mel. Even Sheriff Bergum and Grandma.

I took Mama's crane, wingless still, and set it on the nightstand. I kept noodling with it, and as I noodled, one of the legs fell off. Somehow that helped me see that it didn't have to be a crane after all. I wanted it to be a horse. I took the other leg off and fashioned four new ones. Then attached a proper head to the long, dignified neck. I cut a faded aluminum can into strips for a tail and mane. It had known what it was even if I hadn't. Mrs. Snickels had wanted us to make something we were passionate about and even though it was still tricky for me to feel that way about anything else, I felt that way about Daisy.

Mama had always said that art was about letting yourself fly. But maybe that was just one way. Sometimes it took digging down deep and planting roots. I figured I might tell that to Mrs. Snickels when I handed the horse in as my final art project. Then she'd know her Observation of the Month prize had truly gone to the right person.

The last thing I hung on my bulletin board was Daddy's poem.

A solitary bird, hollow it flew
Through a haze of months marked by the moon
Come to a meadow, shiny with dew
Where hollow bones sang, and deep inside grew
The secret hum of a daisy in June.

The poem was dated after my grandparents had died in the fire, when my father had come to live with Margery. I'd been thinking about it, and maybe Auburn Valley was the meadow, shiny with dew. To me, the poem was about possibility. It was about the secret hum of a daisy.

The secret hum of home.

Acknowledgments

A first book is so very fragile when it comes into the world, like little Daisy on her newborn legs. There is lots of falling down before there is standing up. Here are the amazing people who have given their time, love, and commitment to both Grace and me:

Heartfelt thanks go to my indefatigable writers' group, who has read this story at least one million times, helping shape it every step of the way. It's been a wonderful twelve years and I'm looking forward to the next twelve: Georgia Bragg, Leslie Margolis, Anne Reinhard, Christine Bernardi, Victoria Beck, Cathleen Young, Elizabeth Passarelli, and Rebecca Mohan—we have to make sure our kids deposit us into the same retirement community so we can continue to read to each other, laugh, and eat tons of hummus.

For the friends who have read versions of the story, and for those who haven't but have provided tentpoles in other ways: Amanda Winn Lee, Julene Summers, Judith Whitaker, and Sara Larkins. I miss our weekly Goddess meetings, but you are here with me when I write. Every day. Diana Greenwood—you never doubted. Smooches.

To Nan Marino, who has talked me through the whole publication journey, answering all my pesky questions. Thanks for reminding me to harness the fear and use it as energy. I will keep that with me always. And may that swanky New York bar vanish from our minds.

A special thanks to the Society of Children's Book Writers and Illustrators and Sue Alexander for the Sue Alexander Award. Before she died, Sue was so very encouraging, and the SCBWI has been an ongoing source of learning and inspiration. I can't say enough about the tremendous resources you provide for writers and illustrators. So many of us are where we are because of you.

To Kent Brown, Patti Gauch, and the Highlights Foundation, without whose generous support I would not have been able to attend Chautauqua and have Patti as my manuscript advisor. My journey as a writer began on a picnic bench under the lush green leaves where I learned that character was the heart of a story.

To Rosemary Stimola, who may or may not understand how important lightning-fast responses are to a neurotic writer. So thanks for lightning-fast e-mails, unwavering confidence, and professionalism. It was nearly impossible for me not to believe in myself with you by my side.

And Stacey Barney. Your considerate thoughts and questions nurtured this manuscript into a book. Thanks for pushing me to dig deeper into my characters and their relationships, for patiently asking all the right questions, and for answering mine as many times as it took until I understood. I can't imagine a world without the thoughtful care and love that editors pour into their books, and I certainly can't imagine my writing world without you in it.

Also to Cindy Howle, Sharon Beck, and Janet Robbins, who copyedited and proofread like friends. I wish they could follow me around in my life and edit as necessary. And Annie Ericsson, thank you for such a gorgeous cover. Those lovely birds are what I see when I think of my story.

Mom. Thank you for being my number one fan, and for telling me I was a great writer every step of the way. I don't know about the "great" part. But I can finally call myself a writer. Thanks for saving all my scraps and poems, which kept the fire burning even when my life took another path for a while. Everyone should have someone like you in their lives.

Kevin. Husband, Hero, and Master Brainstormer. Thank you for being a soft place to land when I needed it, and a butt-kicker when I didn't. You are my very best friend and the love of my life. I promise to torture you with writing questions for the rest of your life.

Kate, Sara, and Maddy. There would be no book without you. I'm certain of it. Because of each of you, I have the right words. Mothering you has given me purpose and inspiration. You are the lights of my life.